Puffin Books

HENRY'S LEG

Henry Hooper has a few problems with his life: his dad has left home for a new girlfriend and his mum has almost given up looking after him, his school uniform is half a dozen sizes too small and everyone laughs at him for collecting junk to keep in his bedroom. Everyone, that is, except for the local thugs when they see that Henry has picked up a plastic leg from a fashion dummy. For some reason a series of sinister goings-on seem associated with the leg and a lot of sinister people suddenly want it! Henry wasn't looking for adventure – he preferred the quiet life; but like it or not he finds himself at the centre of a real-life mystery, and all because of a plastic leg.

Funny, lovable Henry also finds himself in yet another comedy thriller: that of his rather complicated life. But with excitement, humour and a marvellously vivid cast of characters, *Henry's Leg* is a gripping read.

Winner of the 1986 *Guardian* Award for Children's Fiction.

Ann Pilling hails from the north of England, where *Henry's Leg* is set. She has written several novels for children under the name of Anne Cheetham. She lives in Oxford, and is married with two sons.

Another book by Ann Pilling
THE YEAR OF THE WORM

ANN PILLING

Henry's Leg

Illustrated by Rowan Clifford

PUFFIN BOOKS

Puffin Books, Penguin Books Ltd, Harmondsworth, Middlesex, England
Viking Penguin Inc., 40 West 23rd Street, New York, New York 10010, U.S.A.
Penguin Books Australia Ltd, Ringwood, Victoria, Australia
Penguin Books Canada Limited, 2801 John Street, Markham, Ontario, Canada L3R 1⬤
Penguin Books (N.Z.) Ltd, 182–190 Wairau Road, Auckland 10, New Zealand

First published by Viking Kestrel 1985
Published in Puffin Books 1986

Made and printed in Great Britain by
Hazell Watson & Viney Limited,
Member of the BPCC Group,
Aylesbury, Bucks
Typeset in Palatino

For Joe,
with love always

9   I want! I want!

Pub.d by W Blake 17 May 1/93

Illustration by William Blake from his book *For Children: The Gates of Paradise*, originally published in 1793.

1

When Henry Hooper got in from school he usually had a big
bowl of cornflakes. Today it was a bigger bowl than normal
and he was shovelling down the spoonfuls like a man stoking
a boiler.

'Henry! I know you've got a big mouth but there's no need
to eat like a pig at a trough is there?' That's what his mother
would have said, if she'd been at home. She wasn't though
– she was out as usual, and she'd not left him a note or
anything.

He was feeling miserable; that's why he sat scoffing
cornflakes. He hadn't been to school anyway; he'd been up
the road in Nev Hodgkinson's shed. The new term didn't
start till Tuesday morning but it was already Monday afternoon. Henry didn't like school very much, and the sands of
time were running out rapidly. That was another reason he
felt gloomy.

The summer had been a washout. His mother had been
cheerful enough because there'd been plenty of work to do.
People had kept going off on holiday and she had been very
busy for six weeks, clattering away on her typewriter at the
kitchen table, or going into Darnley to help out in someone's
office. Henry had spent a week in a seaside caravan with his
dad and Sheila Howarth, the new girlfriend.

It was Sheila's own idea – she'd sent him a letter and asked
him – but it hadn't worked out. They'd had to share the
caravan with her married sister and a new baby, and it was
too much of a squash. The baby got wind and cried all the
time and it had really irritated Henry's father. He'd shouted
at Sheila, and she'd shouted at Henry, for treading sand all

over the caravan floor. She hadn't much liked the interesting pieces of rubbish he'd brought home from the beach either, or the crabs he'd left in the sink. They were perfectly safe, in a red bucket, but she still went on about it. She was supposed to be marrying Dad too, eventually. Wicked stepmother wouldn't be in it then. Henry'd stay at home, with his mum.

He couldn't understand why his Dad liked Sheila. She'd been all right to begin with but now she'd become obsessed with clean floors and personal hygiene. In a few years she'd be just like Eunice Snell.

The Snell family lived next door to the Hoopers in the last house on the Springfield Executive Development. Mr Snell was a house agent and when they'd built the split-level bungalows his firm had sold them off one by one. They had the most superior house on the estate, and the best view. Just so long as they kept their eyes averted from Fir Grove.

Fir Grove belonged to the Hoopers. It was big and gloomy-looking, all on its own at the edge of the Executive Development, and it was over a hundred years old. It stood forlornly at the end of a long drive, in the middle of a great jungle garden. Henry's dad used to cut the hedges now and again, and do the odd bit of pruning, but Ivy Hooper never touched it. At the back it was like a little forest. Tarzan might come swinging out of the undergrowth any minute on his rope of creepers.

Henry was fond of Fir Grove. 'In the olden days people would have come up that drive in carriages,' his father used to tell him when he was little. The drive was full of pot-holes now, and all the flower-beds produced was broken bricks and chip papers. It had got even more run-down since Dad had walked out; Henry's mother just didn't seem to care any more, not without his dad there. But Henry still didn't want to live anywhere else, though Mr Snell was always advising his mother to sell up.

Dad had moved out last year; he'd got Sheila and Mum had got Fir Grove. It had become very decrepit very quickly after that because she'd had to go out to work. There was no money to see to things like leaking gutters and peeling paint, and no time either.

Eunice Snell always had plenty of time. She kept dropping

hints about the thistles and dandelion seeds that floated over from the Hoopers' garden and ruined her lawn, and she was always hacking at their dangling climbers with big secateurs. Now she'd got Frankie to look after Henry thought she might cool off a bit, and stop nagging, but she still spied on them. The Snells must be the most organized family in Darnley, and their Frankie the most organized baby.

The cornflakes packet was empty but Henry was still famished. Why was there never anything to eat in this house? He found bread and margarine and began to make himself a tomato sauce sandwich. Dinner had been a sandwich too, a very small one. No wonder his insides were meeting in the middle. Mum had promised him something good for tea tonight, but so far there were no interesting cooking smells drifting from the oven. It'd be bacon and eggs again, or they'd go and have chips in Jubilee Road. He was starting to look like a chip.

Suddenly Henry remembered where his mother was. She'd gone over to Bell Street Juniors for some school uniform, at the last minute as usual. All the other parents had bought it in July when they'd been told. This special sale was only for people who'd been 'unavoidably absent' first time around, and for new parents.

'Well I forgot,' she'd said rather sheepishly when Henry complained that he'd be walking round school in his vest and underpants. 'I don't approve of this uniform lark anyway, not when you're going to the Comprehensive next year. That's why I forgot, Henry; it was psychological.'

He could see her point. Making the older ones have uniform was silly really, and it would never have happened if Bell Street Juniors hadn't been merged with Oakdene Primary because of 'falling rolls'. That's when the rot had set in.

Henry had quite liked school before the bossy brigade arrived. They'd kept Bell Street open because it was bigger; the Oakdene mothers didn't like it at all but there was nothing they could do. So they'd got up a parents' committee and now they were busy trying to change everything in sight. Uniform, for example, they'd always had a uniform at Oakdene. 'It does raise the tone of the school,' a Mrs Lilian Pargetter had confided to Mrs Snell. 'And there's no need to buy anything new of course – we'll fix up a sale of second-hand stuff, for the poorer ones.'

Her son Jonathan was a real drip. He came from Beeswood, a leafy suburb with moorland views in the poshest part of Darnley. He was learning the flute and his school shorts came down to his ankles. Who wanted to be like Jonathan Pargetter?

As Henry sat glumly chewing his sandwich something was pushed through the letterbox. He wandered down the hall and picked a newspaper off the door mat. It was the *Darnley Star*, the local free paper, out every Monday and full of terrific bargains. Not that Henry could buy any at the moment – he was skint.

He'd worked out that his pocket money (when his mother remembered) must be two thirds below the national average and he'd just invested it in a pair of gerbils from Nev Hodgkinson. 'When they produce,' Nev had explained 'which will be any time now, you can go down to the pet shop with them and they'll give you 50p for the babies.'

'50p *each*?'

'Yes, yes I think so. It'll soon tot up anyway, then you'll be rolling.' Nev had been dead keen to sell Henry those gerbils.

Well, there were no signs yet. The male was enormous and spent all its time guzzling in a corner and going to sleep; the female was thin and anxious-looking and ran up and down the cage ten times a minute, shivering and twitching. Nev didn't give his animals names – he was always on the make and he had a very quick turnover. He'd got rabbits now anyway.

But Henry felt that pets weren't human unless you called them something. After some thought he'd christened the fat one Big Daddy and the thin one Eunice Snell.

Rolled up inside the *Darnley Star* was a sheaf of advertisements. One was from the Bingo Palace in Rochdale Road. 'This way to Fun and Fortune' it said. 'It's not your money we want, it's your friendship.' Pull the other one, thought Henry, screwing it up. Another came from a local building society. It featured a fat boy in a dunce's cap sitting on a great pile of money bags. 'Be a financial wizard at sixteen,' it urged him.

Some hopes. Henry made a ball of it and chucked it into

the bin after Fun and Fortune. A big glossy leaflet from Kelly's Kitchen Showrooms looked rather more promising. 'Write a two-line slogan about Kelly Products', it suggested, 'and win the kitchen of your dreams.'

Henry looked round the kitchen of Fir Grove with its green paint, its crumbly damp walls, its cooker that should be in a museum. They could use a dream kitchen. If this place was smartened up a bit his mother might stop threatening to move. Every time rain came through the roof, or another bit of the fence collapsed, she went into a mood and began talking to Mr Snell. Dad had always been promising to do the kitchen up but he'd never got round to it. That was the kind of thing they were always arguing about.

Henry stuffed the brochure in his pocket and started to read the free paper. The back page was the best with its 'Nothing More Than a Pound' column. He was a great collector of junk and he'd found some cracking bargains in the *Star*. Not lately though. Now all the typists were back from their holidays his mother was 'between jobs' again.

A little notice, all on its own in a black frame, suddenly caught his eye. 'HEDGEHOGS REQUIRED: Dead hedgehogs are needed by research zoologist Keith Barraclough who would like them put into polythene bags and deep frozen before contacting him at the Borough Road Polytechnic, Darnley 56711. Good prices paid.'

Henry read it twice then went down the hall and picked the phone up. What would a 'good price' be, for a really big hedgehog? It had to be better than 50p for one of Eunice Snell's gerbil babies. Research scientists were paid quite a lot these days.

He dialled the first two numbers then put the receiver down again. What if the man asked him how old he was, and where he'd be getting the hedgehogs from? There might be a few snags if he had to go into details. He ought to get a few first, and take them to the Poly in person. The hedgehogs themselves were no problem – Henry could get hedgehogs any day. But freezing them might be more difficult; this scientist wanted them *deep* frozen.

It was no good using their fridge, it was on its last legs; the door wouldn't stay shut and the tiny freezing compartment had no door at all. When his mother wanted to get something really cold she always put it under the window in the front room. Henry was stumped.

He rolled up the *Star* and went back into the kitchen to throw it away. Then he thought of something. The Snells were freezer people. Next door it was frozen pizza for dinner and frozen cod-in-a-bag for tea. Mrs Snell had a craze for freezing things and she didn't always defrost in time. She'd once invited Henry to tea and they'd had crunchy ham sandwiches with ice in the middle. They'd got *two* freezers, a big one in their kitchen and an even bigger one in the garage. That was the one to go for.

Henry went out of the back door and plunged into his jungle garden. If their Graham was playing out on the lawn he could have a quiet word with him.

2

He went half-way down the garden and scrambled up into an old lilac tree. It leaned right over the fence and gave him a perfect view of Snells'. The neat square lawn on the other side was bright green and curiously flat, as though someone had been over it with a vacuum cleaner.

Mrs Snell hoovered everything in sight. Every single morning she went charging round the house, the minute their Frankie had gone to sleep in his pram. This lawn looked as if it had been manicured with scissors – there wasn't a grass blade out of place and in the brown weedless borders everything was planted in tidy rows, with the flowers all standing up to attention. It was a really boring garden in Henry's opinion, not a patch on theirs.

'Psst!' he whispered through the leaves. 'Hey, Graham! Are you doing anything? Do you want to come over?'

Graham Snell was startled and spun round. He'd been standing in the middle of the lawn, peacefully playing swing-ball and missing every time. He was no good at games and his arms were all stringy and thin like his mother's. He had funny ears too, very pink and a bit crumpled at the edges, like one of Nev Hodgkinson's rabbits. He looked very professional though, in his crisp blue shorts and his dazzling white T-shirt; he was obviously all set for the Olympics. No second-hand uniform for him.

'All new for our Graham,' Mrs Snell had told Henry's mother over the fence. 'We can sell it back next summer, if he looks after it.' There was a chair in his bedroom covered with sickly pink roses. 'I've promised him that when he's married,' she informed visitors, 'provided he's careful with it.'

13

All the Snells had one eye on the future and that chair still looked brand new. It was hideous and Henry wouldn't have touched it with a barge-pole. He had a red sag-bag to sit on, up in his attic.

'Come over,' he urged through the lilac branches. Graham Snell was in his class at school. They weren't exactly bosom friends – most of the time they merely tolerated one another through the creepers – but it'd be fatal to fall out with him just at the moment. Snell co-operation was vital in the hedgehog project.

Graham had dropped his bat and yards of elastic, with a pink ball on the end, were steadily wrapping themselves

round his neck. Henry peered in fascination through the branches as the boy tried to untangle himself. He wasn't making a very good job of it, he'd be strangled in a minute. 'Well, are you coming?' he repeated, when the ball and elastic lay tidily on the lawn again with the bat placed neatly beside them. Henry was single-minded when he'd got plans.

Graham Snell hesitated. His mother didn't like him playing at Hoopers' in case he got dirty. But that enormous attic bedroom with its great collection of junk really fascinated him, and he'd only been up there twice.

'All right,' he said slowly. 'But I won't be able to stay very long. Mum's down at the baby clinic with our Frankie.' He had a thin, wobbly sort of voice, just like his mother's. He was a boy Eunice really, Henry decided. The baby on the other hand looked more like its dad, fleshy and fat with a smooth round head like a pink balloon, and a huge letter box mouth. Sometimes, when he had a tantrum, the great red slit opened in a roar. Mrs Snell suffered from 'nerves'. When Frankie screamed she put his pram at the bottom of the garden and shut all the windows.

'Hey! I thought you were coming over?' Henry shouted.

'I am, but I'll come down the drive. Let me in at the front will you.'

Honestly. He did a quick Tarzan leap out of the lilac tree and pushed his way through the tangled shrubbery towards Fir Grove. Any self-respecting boy would have squeezed through the fence. There were enough holes in it.

A notice on the bedroom door said 'Darnley Tip'. Henry tried to push past, into the attic, but Graham had spotted it and stood there staring, with a silly grin on his face.

'Who did that then, Henry?'

'My mum. She thinks this room's a bit of a mess.'

Mess wasn't the word. There was twice as much junk as last time, and Henry was obviously running out of space. As well as all the tea-chests and cardboard boxes he'd got things piled up in corners now and heaped up on window-sills, queer things like a million wire coat-hangers tied together with string, and the insides of about two million toilet rolls. Henry Hooper was peculiar.

'Where do you sleep?' said Graham. There was no sign of a bed.

'Over here, under the window,' grunted Henry, pointing to what looked like the corner of a mattress, more or less buried under a heap of shoe-boxes.

'Don't you have a proper bed then?'

'No. Not now. I did have.'

'What happened to it?'

'Oh, it collapsed,' Henry explained, feeling vaguely foolish. Then he added enthusiastically. 'It's good sleeping on a floor. It's good for your back.'

But Graham Snell didn't look at all convinced. What if mice crawled over you in the middle of the night? Or spiders? There'd be both in a place like this, it *was* a tip.

Henry was starting to feel rather uncomfortable. He shouldn't have invited Graham Snell up here. He just stood there gawping in his flashy Olympic shorts, asking a lot of silly questions. It was quite obvious that he thought Henry was a nutcase. He was no doubt thinking about his own neat room at home with its Superman wallpaper and its posters of Common British Birds, not forgetting The Chair.

The attic might look a mess to an outsider, but in its own weird way it was quite organized. Henry Hooper was an organized boy. All his boxes were carefully labelled in felt-tip. 'Copper and Brass' Graham Snell spelled out, his watery blue eyes roving round, 'Miscellaneous', 'Electrical' and 'Second World War'. Most of the stuff in that one had come from the Army Surplus Store in town. They'd got some real bargains in that shop. His mum had bought him his gas-mask from there, on his last birthday.

'What do you *want* all this stuff for, Henry?' she'd said on the birthday morning, handing over the gas-mask, all done up in Snoopy paper. And that's what Graham Snell was saying now. 'What d'you keep it all for? It can't be worth much.'

'Oh, it'll come in,' said Henry. That was all he ever said. He didn't always know why he wanted things; he just wanted them. So he picked stuff off rubbish tips and out of dustbins before the refuse lorries came round. People threw the most amazing things away sometimes, really good tins, with lids

16

on, and pieces of copper tubing, and old irons that still worked. Henry brought stuff like that home quite often and carried it upstairs to his attic.

One thing he'd always fancied was the biggest organ pipe in Nelson Street Chapel where his gran went. Wanting that great silver pipe was Henry's earliest memory. But how could you explain something like that to Graham Snell? He'd think you were barmy.

He was already looking anxiously through the window, Henry noticed, pink ears pricked for sounds of Mother's Return. Mr Snell was picking them up from the clinic so he'd hear the car first. At the least noise from outside Graham quaked slightly, and waited for Frankie to start yelling down in the garden. If his mum discovered where he was she'd wipe the floor with him. She disapproved of him playing at Henry Hooper's; she thought he'd get germs.

'Fabulous view, isn't it?' said Henry. You could see everything from up here – the Rec with its battered goal posts, the Darnley Canal, and the ruin of Spring Mill with its two great chimneys. Behind were the grey-green moors, slashed in two by the new motorway extension as it ribboned its way across the hills to Leeds. Henry loved that view. His dad used to take him up on those moors at weekends, looking for buried mineshafts and the old, forgotten Roman road. Sheila Howarth's arrival had ended all that. Henry missed those walks a lot.

All Graham could see was rotting window frames and cracked glass. The house was a wreck. If only his father could persuade Henry's mother to sell up, Clutterbuck and Sadler could pull it down and develop the land. The firm might become Clutterbuck, Sadler and *Snell* then. But Ivy Hooper was a funny woman. One minute she was all for getting rid of Fir Grove, the next minute she loved it.

Plotting the Hoopers' next move drove Mrs Snell berserk. She said she didn't like living next door to an overgrown scrap-yard. If the Hoopers were still there in six months, she said, she was moving. You didn't get people like Ivy Hooper in Beeswood.

Mr Snell, who was a quiet, reasonable sort of man, though rather obsessed with becoming a partner in his estate agent's business, was always trying to make his wife see sense about the Hoopers, but she just wouldn't listen.

'They've always lived in a tip,' she said. '*Always*. Long before the break-up. You know they have, George.'

'But Henry's all right, love,' Mr Snell pleaded mildly. 'He's a kind-hearted sort of boy, do anything for anyone that sort would. And, well, just think what he's been through . . .'

Eunice sniffed. 'Huh.' She wasn't at all sure whether a boy like that was a good influence on their Graham, a boy who filled his room with smelly rubbish, just *picked up*, off the *street*. All right, she did feel sorry for him, the dad running off with a young woman and abandoning him to that scatty mother, all his patched-up worn-through clothes and his unwashed hair. But there *were standards*.

'Make me a cup of tea, love,' she said suddenly, in rather a different tone. She'd seen a nice semi for sale in Linden Avenue, Beeswood, and she wanted to 'talk' to George about it.

Meanwhile, in next door's attic, Henry was conducting some delicate negotiations. When the freezer was brought into the conversation Graham was definitely suspicious, and Henry had to use bribes to get what he wanted. He was like his father, he never did anything for nothing. That was how you got on.

'What do you want it for?' he kept saying. You'd have thought Henry was planning to steal it, TV dinners and all, and hide it in his attic. All he wanted was a couple of cubic feet for a few hedgehogs. But he couldn't tell Graham that.

'It's just something I'm working on,' he said vaguely. 'I've got to freeze something hard. Look, they're – it's not very big, and I'll wrap it up properly. It won't be for long anyway. Come on, Graham.'

After a bit of wheedling the puzzled Olympic champ agreed to hide Henry's mystery item under the sprouts. His mother had done a bulk buy on them last winter, and it was still sprouts with everything. There were bags and bags of them in the garage freezer, and no danger of reaching the bottom yet.

If Henry stuffed his package out of sight, under Mr Snell's workbench in the garage, Graham promised to deal with it when his mother was out of the way. In return he got some stuff for his model railway – twelve polystyrene tiles to cut up into houses and a big lump of green foam rubber to make trackside woodland.

Graham Snell's idea of fun was to watch his little trains whizz round and round a track. Big thrill, Henry thought gloomily, handing over his treasures. Those tiles were new as well. It was quite a price to pay for storing a few frozen hedgehogs, and he'd not even got them yet.

3

When Henry got a really good idea he always wanted to act immediately, but morning was the best time for hedgehogs so he planned to have an early night and slip out next day before school. His mother made him late going to bed though; she wanted to see him in his uniform.

'I look stupid,' he grumbled, scowling at himself in her spotty bedroom mirror. 'Look at these, Mum, they're miles too small.'

'Well, I told you, you should have come with me, then I wouldn't have had to guess the size.'

'These' were a pair of little purple shorts. *Purple*, the whole outfit was purple, more or less: mauve shirt, maroon socks, and a scratchy shapeless blazer made of sickly reddish cloth. The colour reminded him of stewed prunes. Now his dad would never have let him go to school looking like that; they'd have had a row about it. He looked a real sight.

'Don't *frown*, Henry,' his mother said mildly, ignoring his complaints. He always went on about things. 'If the wind changes you'll stay like that, and you've got a nice face.'

Henry didn't agree. He secretly thought he was funny-looking. His face was big, just like a clown's, and everything about it was slightly comical. He had a curly mouth, a stubby blunt nose, light-brown eyes set miles apart and the kind of skin that went brown easily. In summer he got covered in freckles, thousands of them, running together like the blobs on the top of Horlicks. Everyone knew about Henry Hooper's freckles, he looked as if he'd been sunbathing through a tea-strainer. He had problems with his hair too. There was plenty of it, but a clump on top always stuck straight up, as if it was startled.

Mrs Hooper took a good look at him and wished she'd done rather better with the uniform. He was popping out of it on all sides. But when she'd arrived at the school nearly everything had gone. Henry was so *large*, he looked older than eleven, with his spade-like hands, his great feet, his legs like little tree-trunks. Whichever way you looked at it he really didn't look his best in shorts.

'I look *ridiculous*,' he said hotly, just as if he'd been reading her mind. 'I'll get laughed at, Mum. I feel like staying away tomorrow.'

'Oh, you'll be all right, love,' she murmured, as if saying that solved all the problems in the world. 'Everyone's gone second-hand, except Snells of course.' She was more interested in putting rollers in her hair. 'I'm going after a new job tomorrow afternoon anyway. If I get it we could go out on the town.'

But Henry had stopped listening. Good jobs were hard to come by and he'd heard it all before. They were in for a lean time. He was already climbing up his attic stairs, unbuttoning the sickly pink shirt as he went.

'Good night, love,' his mother called after him, but he didn't answer. He was trying to remember where he'd put that alarm clock that he'd found in a dustbin in Jubilee Road.

At half past six the next morning he was pedalling along the canal towpath on his ancient fairy-cycle. He was wearing his hedgehog outfit – old jeans, sneakers and the Darnley Joggers sweatshirt he'd bought at a jumble sale. He wasn't going to put that purple uniform on till the very last minute.

It had been all laid out on a chair when he woke up; his mother must have crept in last night and done it. Henry usually got his own clothes ready, so she was obviously feeling guilty about leaving everything to the eleventh hour.

His fairy-cycle was the laugh of the neighbourhood. It had curly old-fashioned handlebars, thick heavy mudguards and a peculiar narrow seat that pinched his bottom. It looked pre-war. Henry had once owned a proper bike, like everyone else on the estate, a Raleigh Winner. His dad had bought it for his eleventh birthday. But it had only lasted a week. On the first Saturday morning he'd rushed back from Nev's to watch

Multi-Coloured Swap Shop and left it outside the gate. And it had been pinched. People were always nicking things in Darnley.

His mother had wiped the floor with him. There'd been a padlock and chain to lock it up with, but Henry had forgotten. For weeks he'd walked everywhere, then Nev Hodgkinson's dad turned up with this fairy-cycle. He was a bit of a mystery, Nev's dad was; he was always 'finding' things that had accidentally dropped off lorries.

He liked Henry Hooper though and he knew how much the boy missed his dad. He could see it in his eyes when they all sat round the Hodgkinsons' tea table, with the twins throwing bread and jam at each other.

Henry didn't mind about the fairy-cycle being old-fashioned but he did mind being laughed at, so he only rode round on it when no one was looking. He should try and win a bike as well as a dream kitchen, he decided, as he trundled past Spring Mill. It was the only way he'd ever get a new one.

The new dual carriageway that led to the M62 was the best place for hedgehogs. He'd been along it very early with his dad and Sheila Howarth, on the way to the caravan, and he'd noticed then how many things had been squashed during the night. The hedgehogs obviously couldn't be too squashed, not if the man at the Poly was going to dissect them, but this was definitely the place. What he needed to look out for were things that had been given a little knock on the head, then crept off to die.

There was a footbridge over the dual carriageway. Henry stood in the middle and looked down. Quite a few cars were whopping past already but he could see promising dark patches here and there. He unhooked his plastic carrier bag from the handle of the fairy-cycle and began to walk along the side of the road, with one eye open for hedgehogs and the other for police cars. He didn't want to get stopped.

The first thing he saw was a dead cat. He felt quite sick for a minute, he liked cats. He approached it cautiously, hoping it wasn't anybody he knew. Hodgkinsons had two cats and they kept having kittens. Graham Snell had asked for one once but his mother wouldn't let him; she said cats could give you fleas.

22

Henry must have spent a good half hour walking up and down that road. Three night-crawlers had met a sticky end in the slow lane but they'd been so well flattened they'd ended up like fur gloves. They were probably rabbits anyway. In the end he ran out of time. He was plodding back to his bicycle, his carrier empty and his stomach rolling, when he spotted a hedgehog right under his nose, quite a fat one, all ripe for the picking.

He rolled it over with his foot, then bent down and poked at it. It was all pink and spongy underneath and it was definitely dead. There wasn't much blood on it though. He knelt down and had a closer look. Its little face was quite perfect, wizened and calm-looking, like the face of a very old man. Henry felt rather sorry for it; it wasn't fair on animals.

If he'd not enlisted help from Graham Snell he might well have left it where it was, but Graham knew something was up now, and Henry didn't want to lose face. Anyway, he needed the cash. It was a big hedgehog in good condition. The man at the Poly could easily give him a pound for it.

He scooped it up with his old trowel and put it carefully into the carrier bag, but all the time one dead little eye was staring at him. Henry looked away. He was being daft. This hedgehog might lead to a cure for some deadly disease; it was only like giving your body to science.

4

Henry and Graham usually went to school together, collecting the Hodgkinsons on the way. It wasn't ideal but Mrs Snell thought there was safety in numbers, and she didn't like their Graham crossing main roads on his own. The Snells had the smartest house on the estate and the Hodgkinsons had the shabbiest. Nev's parents were rather easy-going. They had five children and a front garden full of dismembered cars. They were another reason for moving to Beeswood.

At ten past eight the hedgehog was safely hidden under the sprouts and the two boys stood outside Nev's front door. Graham's uniform was brand new and he was looking unbelievably pink and clean, shiny almost, as if he'd been put through a car wash. He was clutching a string bag that contained a new football. Nobody was allowed to play with it yet though, in case it got marks on it.

Henry was bulging out of his clothes. 'You'll have to get me a bigger shirt, Mum,' he'd told his mother at breakfast. 'This collar's killing me.' But Mrs Hooper believed in making do; she could always move the buttons. 'Stick your stomach in,' she suggested helpfully as he trailed off down the drive.

Why don't I just give up breathing, Henry thought glumly, tugging at the collar. He'd be dead before he reached school.

The Hodgkinsons were never ready on time. Graham had to knock twice before there were signs of life then the door suddenly burst open and three children shot out like bullets from a gun – shock-headed Nev Hodgkinson, big and lumpy with his new tie already looking like chewed string, and his twin sisters, Sandra and Susan. They were in Class Three and they squabbled all the time. Nev called them The Ugly Sisters.

Bell Street Juniors was a bus ride down Jubilee Road. Nev and Henry sat at the front upstairs and silently inspected each other's uniforms. Nev looked daft too, all his stuff was several sizes too big and there was a patch on the seat of his purple shorts. It quite comforted Henry. The Ugly Sisters stayed at the back and practised blowing bubbles with pink gum. Graham had a seat to himself, in the middle, and sat stroking his football through its string bag.

As the long red school wall came into view a great gloom fell upon Henry. Last term had been bad enough, with all those clever-clever people in the form from Oakdene Primary, always bringing notes of complaint from their bossy mothers about the way Bell Street was run. But this term there was something much worse in store; they were Top Class Juniors now, they'd be in Class Six. That was when you had The Beast.

The Beast was Miss Sugden, the Deputy Head. She was little and fat with thick stumpy legs and a booming voice. She was called The Beast because she had a moustache, and because she spat when she got excited. You got wet if you sat at the front in Miss Sugden's class.

But when the classroom door opened, Henry had a surprise. The person walking to the teacher's table with a register and a sheaf of papers wasn't The Beast at all. This person was tall and thin and she had clouds of fuzzy gold hair. 'My name's Miss Bingham,' she said with a dazzling smile. 'Do sit down.'

'Where's Miss Sugden then?' Nev called out from the back row. He always said exactly what came into his head. The Beast would have bellowed at him for speaking out of turn, but Miss Bingham merely flashed her very white teeth and said sweetly, 'Oh, she's not here, dear. I'm standing in for her.'

'Where is she?'

Miss Bingham paused. 'She's . . . she's been, er, called to higher things,' she said finally.

'Perhaps she's dead,' Henry muttered hopefully to Graham Snell. The Beast terrified him.

No such luck. She'd only gone on a course, and she was

coming back after Christmas. 'It's a training course,' explained Miss Bingham. 'It's because of the merger.'

Oh heck. What would a Beast Improvement Course do to Miss Sugden? She'd be worse than ever when she got back. Henry was leaving.

On the first day the class teachers always kept their children till break. This gave them an hour and a half for 'form business' and Miss Bingham was obviously going to need every second of it. After about five minutes it became obvious that she couldn't keep order.

People started to whisper, then to chat. The hum gradually grew into a roar. Nev Hodgkinson began to flick ink pellets at the girls by the radiator and the two back rows organized a golf tournament with rubbers and rulers, and an old waste-paper basket. Up at the front the goody-goodies from Oakdene were trying to shush everyone into silence.

Miss Bingham didn't raise her voice. She simply clapped her hands together and said brightly, 'My time, children, my time now. I want to go through the register and learn all your names.'

My time. Henry exchanged looks with Nev. It was like *Playschool*, with Goldilocks up at the front, clapping and smiling. She'd produce Big Ted in a minute.

Doing the register took a long time. It was a large form now, with all the extra people from Oakdene, and nobody stopped talking. When she wasn't clapping her hands and asking for silence Miss Bingham was having friendly little chats as she crawled down the list. Henry was bored. If she didn't hurry up they'd miss Break. Outside it was a mild September morning, windless and warm with a deep blue sky stretched over Darnley. What a day to be stuck in a stuffy classroom.

When she called your name out you had to stand up and be talked to. 'Henry Hooper' the high voice trilled at last. When he got to his feet a button popped off his shirt, whizzed across the room and landed in Mavis Bramley's inkwell. That was three gone, and a yawning gap behind Henry's tie revealed acres of pink stomach. People were laughing.

'Henry Hooper,' Miss Bingham repeated, rolling the name round her mouth. 'Now that's a name to remember. It's a Royal name too, now.'

The front row goody-goodies sniggered and smirked. Everyone knew about Henry and his daft mother, how his dad had walked out one day and gone to live with someone in the town flats, and about Fir Grove and the way he went scavenging in dustbins. He blushed and stared at his feet. Henry was an old-fashioned name; Mrs Snell had once told him that. She couldn't really be a 'lady' because ladies didn't make personal remarks. Anyway, he'd been called Henry after his Grandad Clegg, not after Henry the Eighth.

'Henry's quite a *trendy* name these days,' Miss Bingham twittered faintly, his red face telling her that she'd said the wrong thing. 'I think it's absolutely fabulous anyway. Sit down, dear.'

He didn't feel at all trendy, with his gaping shirt front and his tight little shorts, and that drip Jonathan Pargetter had turned right round and was looking at him. Henry pulled his tongue out and stared longingly into the sunny playground. Meanwhile, Miss Bingham crept down the register.

'Olivia Onions,' she said very slowly. It was a hard name to pronounce.

'On*ions*, actually,' a sharp little voice corrected from the front row. Olivia came from Oakdene. She had a small neat face framed in small neat curls, and she was pale and skinny-looking; inside though she had a steel core. 'It's On*ions*,' she repeated. 'It rhymes with "irons".'

'*Really*?' fluttered Miss Bingham, checking her list. 'Only it says Onions here.'

Olivia Onions went puce. There were suppressed giggles behind her and the Bell Street originals grinned at one another. Good old Goldilocks. Olivia was in league with Jonathan Pargetter. They had desks right under the teacher's nose and their hands were up permanently. They weren't used to being laughed at.

Miss Bingham was busy telling her that there was an Olivia in Shakespeare, and how absolutely fabulous it all was. She was inquiring about her hobbies and the fact that Olivia could play the violin was clearly fabulous too.

'Let's throw this open to discussion,' she said suddenly, slapping the register shut. Henry slumped, five minutes to break and they'd only reached the O's. But music was obviously a passion with Miss Bingham, and she was already full of plans for a school orchestra. It must be the effect of all those letters from the Oakdene mothers.

'Of sorts, of *sorts*,' she repeated anxiously when she heard Bell Street murmurings of 'Can't play anything' and 'It's all right if you come from *Oakdene*.' 'It'll be a band rather than an orchestra, great fun, a bit of everything. Now then, what have we got so far? It could be absolutely *fabulous*.'

The stars of the band were obvious from the start. Olivia would play her violin and Jonathan Pargetter his flute. Mavis Bramley was learning the recorder but she'd only done three pages of Book One. 'Never mind, dear,' Miss Absolutely

Fabulous said cheerfully, scribbling it down. 'You can always tootle away in the background.'

Nev Hodgkinson said there was an old drum in their garage. 'It was our Art's,' he explained. 'It's broken, but you can still get a good noise out of it.' And Graham Snell said he might be able to bring his grandfather's trombone; it was on top of his wardrobe in a case. 'It'll be mine when I'm grown up,' he explained proudly. Together with that chair, Henry was thinking. Trombones were enormous, Graham Snell'd never get a note out of a thing like that. One good blow and he'd probably fall over.

'And what about you, Henry?' Miss Bingham said at last. He looked like a boy full of purpose and he must have good strong lungs. She was hoping for another flute, or a trumpet perhaps. 'Are you musical at all?'

There were various rude noises from the sidelines. Henry Hooper certainly wasn't musical, and his singing voice sounded like a cinder under a door. He was a real groaner. Last term The Beast had banned him from the school choir.

'No,' he said flatly. 'And I can't play an instrument.'

Suddenly a great sadness washed over him and he plumped down abruptly on his chair again, looking into the empty playground but seeing only his dad. Mr Hooper came from a whole family of brass-players; he was good on the cornet and Henry had been going to learn too, till last Christmas.

They'd occasionally gone to brass concerts together, at the Town Hall, and though he loved it the music seemed to upset Dad somehow. Perhaps it was all to do with the past and his favourite Uncle Eddie who'd been killed in an awful accident at work. He'd been a crack horn-player, Uncle Eddie had.

'Well isn't there anything you could bring, dear?'

The large, tow-headed Henry, bulging on all sides out of his skimpy purple uniform, looked sad and far away. He clearly wasn't listening. The break bell was ringing now anyway, and Miss Bingham was consulting her list. She vaguely remembered talk in the staff room about this boy, some family break-up last Christmas, and a rather eccentric mother. She wished now she'd not pressed him; it had only made the other kids laugh and he'd looked more like crying.

Anyway, he quite obviously wasn't interested. But she decided to have one last go. 'Nearly everyone's doing *something*. If we could include the whole form it really would be fabulous.'

Henry's mind ran over the contents of his attic. He brightened suddenly. 'I've got an old washboard,' he said. 'I could play that.'

'*How*?' Olivia Onions asked suspiciously. If she was going to be First Violin she didn't want competition, least of all from Henry Hooper on a washboard.

'I think you use thimbles,' he said slowly. 'I've seen it on the telly. Groups used to do it, didn't they?'

'That's *right*, Henry,' said Miss Bingham, her big teeth flashing encouragement. 'Skiffle groups had them. It's a bit dated perhaps, but why not? It'll give us an old-time flavour. Now bring your instruments next Monday,' she said, whizzing from O to Z in about ten seconds flat. 'The area music director's coming then, and he'll advise us.'

In the playground the Oakdene brigade had gone into a huddle to talk about the new band. 'Not a *real* orchestra,' Olivia was saying sniffily. 'And I'm not sure my teacher'll let me, not with all my exam work and everything.'

Henry couldn't really see it getting off the ground anyway; for a start, Mavis Bramley could only play 'Jinglebells'. He could just imagine it, Olivia scraping away on her violin, the golden flute of Jonathan Pargetter, and Graham Snell busting a gut as he tried to get a note out of his grandad's trombone. It could be murder.

He wasn't at all sure that he'd bring his washboard and thimbles next week. They were worth money anyway; it'd be a waste.

5

His mother was out again when he got home that afternoon.
There was no message, no food, no anything, and Henry felt
like crying. There were always things to talk about on the
first day of term. Today there was The Beast's disappearance
and the arrival of Miss Bingham; there was the school band
as well, and the sponsored cycle ride for charity. They'd all
been given leaflets about it at half past three.

It was to raise money for the Darnley Miners' Home.
Grandad Clegg had been a miner and Henry had decided that
this might persuade his mother to get him a new bike. He
couldn't very well raise money for charity on a pre-war fairy-
cycle.

There was nothing in for tea. Henry was rooting about
among some old biscuit tins in the pantry when the phone
rang in the hall. It'd be Mum, with some tale of disaster.

The caller was obviously in a coin box and he waited
patiently for the pips to finish. Last time she'd done this it
was to tell him that the floor had dropped out of the car and
that she was stranded. She had a scooter now, and that was
falling apart too. Perhaps it had given up the ghost in Darnley
town centre.

Dad had always looked after the car; he liked tinkering with
engines. Henry missed him. If only he hadn't gone off with
Sheila Howarth things would be much easier all round. His
mother wouldn't be chasing jobs all the time and the house
wouldn't be falling to pieces. Sheila didn't seem to make his
father very happy anyway, not if that caravan holiday was
anything to go by.

'*Henry!*' his mother was yelling down the phone. 'I'm job-hunting, love. Listen, I've got to stay in town till seven o'clock, the boss can't see me till then. Do you want to go to your gran's? I can pick you up.'

'No,' said Henry. He felt rebellious. It was boring at Gran's and his mother would be hours late collecting him; she was never on time for anything. Dad was the punctual one.

'*What*, love?' The line was crackly.

'*No*,' Henry repeated doggedly. 'I've got homework and I was going over to Nev's later. I'll stay in.'

'All right, chick.' The pips were going now. All Henry heard was 'kettle', 'Tarzan' and 'fish and chips'; then they were cut off. She'd have run out of change of course; she always did.

Henry interpreted the message. There'd be money in the copper kettle on top of the kitchen dresser. He climbed up and found it, some grubby pound notes all screwed together. It was for a fish-and-chip supper and a trip to the cinema. Henry Hooper was God's gift to the cinema industry – he was always being packed off to the Essoldo in Jubilee Road. But he had no intention of going to the new Tarzan film tonight, Dad had taken him to that in Manchester when it first came out. The cinema visits didn't happen any more, but no one had explained it to Henry. He suspected Sheila Howarth though. On Saturday afternoons she went visiting her sister and the new baby, according to Grandma Clegg, and Dad got dragged along too. That'd be the reason, though nobody had ever bothered to inform *him*. It was only his life.

He sat at the kitchen table and fiddled with a few breakfast crumbs. The house was cold and echoey and he felt very hungry, but somehow not for food. Next door Graham Snell would be cosily installed in front of his TV screen (24-inch colour with remote control, and video at the ready for outstanding programmes). Down the road the Hodgkinsons would be viewing too, Sandra and Susan fighting on the settee, Nev belting them periodically, and a baby yelling somewhere in the background. Henry felt lonely now. He was out in the cold at Fir Grove.

He unzipped his school bag and rummaged about for a pencil. Miss Absolutely Fabulous wasn't all froth and bubble, she'd given them homework on the very first night, two whole pages to write on 'My Ambition'. They'd discussed it in class and made notes. Henry opened his rough book.

'Point One,' he'd written. 'Does money make you happy?' Well, it was hard to say – he didn't know any rich people. The Snells were quite well off but they weren't exactly cheerful. Mrs Snell disapproved of everything and was always going on about having an extension, or moving to Beeswood. Graham was a bit of a grabber too, he'd no sooner got his new Raleigh Solo than he wanted a BMX Mongoose. Mr Snell was so busy selling houses he was never at home, their Frankie screamed all the time, and his mother had to take these nerve pills.

The Oakdene lot were probably rich – you had to be to live in Beeswood – but they didn't seem happy either. Jonathan Pargetter went round telling on people, and Olivia was always demanding her 'rights'. All the same, money must make some things easier. They could certainly do with a bit round here.

'Money', Henry wrote thoughtfully 'might not make you happy, but perhaps it makes being miserable easier to bear.'

Ten minutes later he was still looking at it. His brilliance had fizzled out after that first sentence and he couldn't think what else to put, unless he said that his ambition was to have a new bike and win a dream kitchen for his mother, and that sounded daft somehow. In the end he shut his book and chucked his pencil down on top of it. He could do it tomorrow before school; he'd be up early anyway, collecting hedgehogs.

The money from the kettle would buy him fish and chips, popcorn and a seat at the pictures. If he got a small chips there'd be enough for some chocolate too. Food was comforting sometimes and at least it would be warm in the cinema. As he thought about the evening ahead he perked up slightly.

Up in his attic he changed his comic-cuts school uniform for old cord trousers and his Save the Lancs Canals sweatshirt. Five minutes later he was walking through the estate with his hands in his pockets, whistling quietly to himself, and wondering how he could get into the horror film at the Regal.

The Essoldo was at their end of Jubilee Road and Henry went straight past. His mother was wrong anyway, they weren't showing *Tarzan* at all; it was 'A Season of Cartoon Classics'. He liked cartoons but he wasn't in the mood for them tonight. In any case these were all Popeyes and he'd seen them all before. In fact, if he saw Olive Oyl being rescued from that pit of sharks one more time he'd throw up.

So he plodded on towards the Regal, munching his chips. The main road was very long and straight and led into the town centre; it was lined with shops and all the pavements were awash with rubbish, overflowing dustbins and plastic sacks, and big cartons jam-packed with newspapers and polystyrene waste. It had been put out ready for the men from the Refuse Department. They'd be round at the crack of dawn tomorrow, waking everyone up with that big rusty grinder that chewed it all to bits. He'd forgotten it was Tuesday, the day he usually went souvenir-hunting in Jubilee Road.

He was tempted to skip the cinema and to spend his time looking for treasures. But although it was early the sky had become quite dark and he felt a few spots of rain. He'd come out without his anorak and if the heavens opened he'd get soaked. Besides, there was nothing worth investigating this week. After a slow walk past the dustbins he found nothing of interest except a bag of rusty washers and an old tap.

Henry knew why the pickings were lean; he'd just seen his rival, Desperate Dan, stumping off home with two bulging carrier bags. Mrs Snell said Danny Crompton was a filthy old tramp and that if he came hanging round their house again she'd get the police. But he wasn't a tramp; he lived in a back-street near the canal, and he was friends with all the local scrap-merchants.

He made his money by picking rubbish over and selling bits and pieces for cash. He'd probably got thousands stashed away. If Desperate Dan was first on the scene, on Tuesdays, there was no point in hanging around. He always got anything worth keeping. He'd probably be a millionaire when he died. That could go into the composition for Miss Bingham.

Graham's dad had once given Desperate Dan a cup of tea and a cigarette in their garage, and Mrs Snell had thrown a fit. She'd said they'd all get infested and why didn't he go up to the hospital and get himself fitted with a proper artificial limb? He looked disgusting with that stump.

The old man's left leg had been blown off in the war. He had a polished wooden peg that went tap-tapping every Tuesday night along Jubilee Road. With his grizzled beard and his peg-leg he looked like an extra from *Treasure Island*. But Mrs Snell didn't see the romance in things and anything slightly out of the ordinary made her snappy and nervous. She said he was a nuisance and that the council ought to do something about it.

As the old man shuffled off into the drizzle Henry quickened his pace. It was raining quite hard and his Canals sweatshirt felt lumpy and cold. The lights of the Regal cinema were just coming into view when he suddenly stopped dead in his tracks. Across the road, outside a dress shop, he saw three big dustbins all lined up neatly for the chewer, and out of the middle one something was sticking straight up. It was a human leg.

The long wet road, with its façades of dreary little shops, felt empty suddenly, and somehow threatening. The side-streets had turned into shadowy canyons where monster cats lurked. The drizzle was becoming a downpour and Henry's hair was plastered to his head. But he didn't even notice. His brain was working overtime and he just stood there goggling. There'd been a murder on Jubilee Road. The body had been hacked into pieces and stuffed into a dustbin outside Alice Modes Fashions.

It was an old-style dress shop, expensive but 'good'. Mrs Snell bought clothes there and she always looked terrible. At least his own mother had a bit of flair, even if she did get most of her things off the market. She could look quite trendy sometimes.

But trendy wasn't the word for Alice Modes. There it was, sandwiched between a betting shop and a run-down news-agents, its two big windows full of pink corsets and middle-aged hats, and there was this leg, in one of its dustbins. Henry crossed the road to have a closer look.

It had obviously come off a fashion model but there was no sign of the rest of the body, no trunk or arms in the gutter, no odd hand lying on the pavement. Just the leg, with its

red toe-nails, pointing straight up at the tin-coloured Darnley sky.

He walked on, very slowly, then stopped and looked back. He quite fancied that leg. He didn't know why, he just wanted it; it was like wanting Nelson Street organ pipe all over again.

If it was still there after the film had finished he might come back and get it; it'd be properly dark then too. Henry didn't much care what people thought about him but there were limits, and he didn't really want to be seen walking down Jubilee Road with a leg under his arm.

6

It was a double bill at the Regal, a thriller called *Murder to Order* and an old horror film called *The Frog That Ate London*. The posters outside looked about as scary as a day trip to Blackpool but both the films were 'Fifteen'. They wouldn't let him in.

Henry peeped inside the foyer. If that dumpy girl with red hair was on she'd probably sell him a ticket. He knew he looked older than his age and he'd got in once before with Nev. She'd not seemed at all bothered; she'd just taken their money and looked the other way, though his mother would kill him if she knew.

But it was the manager tonight, a fat little man with a glossy bald head and black glasses, scooping up the pound notes and shooting tickets at people through a shiny little slit in the counter. Henry's heart failed him; he daren't try it on with the manager.

Then he had a bit of luck. A small queue was shuffling in for the early performance and in the middle he spotted Nev's big brother, Art, with his girlfriend, Lois Spencer. Art owed Henry a favour. He was the mad car mechanic whose rusty spare parts littered Hodgkinsons' front garden and were slowly driving Mrs Snell to drink. Back in the summer Henry had given him a set of spark-plugs and some copper wire for one of his engines – *given* not *sold*. Art was on the dole and his mum took most of his money. She needed it too, he was a very big eater.

'Art,' Henry whispered. 'Art. Can I come in with you and Lois? It's "Fifteen".'

The youth opened his mouth to say No. That bullet-headed

37

manager had once chucked him out of the Regal, for making a row with the lads. He didn't want any more trouble.

'Go on,' wheedled Henry, hoping he'd remember about the spark-plugs. 'Mum's gone after a job, and she's given me money for the pictures.'

Art turned pink and stared feebly at Lois. She shrugged and stared back. 'I don't mind,' she said carelessly. 'I mean, he needn't *sit* with us, need he?' Then she looked down.

The boy hanging on to Art's sleeve was shabbily dressed; his trousers were worn at the knees and there was a rip in his sweatshirt. He was tall and broad-shouldered but his freckled face was young, and rather anxious-looking. Lois felt sorry for him. Boys like that shouldn't be packed off to horror films all on their own. Why wasn't his dad there, if the mother was job-hunting? She had views on children. He didn't know it yet but she was planning to marry Art and have four.

'Oh, come on,' she said, grabbing Henry's hand and giggling slightly. 'And if anybody asks you're fifteen, and with me.'

'Only don't *sit* near us,' Art mumbled in embarrassment as they plunged into the warm darkness.

Henry had no intention of sitting near them, and as soon as they were inside he made his way down to the front. It was Lovers' Row at the back of the Regal anyway; the serious film-goers always sat in the middle.

The Frog That Ate London was pathetic, and the audience laughed its head off all the way through. The monster frog was obviously made of green foam rubber and 'London' looked like one of Graham Snell's Airfix models. Henry could have done a better job himself.

There was one spectacular moment when The Frog got into Westminster Abbey for the Queen's coronation. They'd used some old newsreel film and it got quite interesting, especially when the Archbishop of Canterbury had his head bitten off.

It went over the top after that though – there were just too many dukes and duchesses being torn limb from limb by The Frog, and Henry grew bored. He couldn't concentrate anyway; he was thinking about his leg and wondering whether someone had nicked it. He was also worried in case that fat little manager came round to check up on him. It was rather nerve-racking, sitting there all on his own.

The horror film was accompanied by the usual loud music, but for about five minutes, in the middle, there was a sudden complete hush. The Frog had got into the Underground and was gobbling up the guards on the Bakerloo line, but all in a deadly silence. Henry couldn't work out whether it was deliberate, to add to the suspense, or whether the Regal was having trouble with its projector again. The couples on Lovers' Row started to jeer and throw sweet-papers, but Henry's ears were listening to something quite different. There were odd noises outside.

First there was a bang, then it sounded as if all the dustbins in Darnley were being rolled round and round inside a huge tin can. He was puzzled. The Refuse Department didn't come round with the grinder till Wednesday morning and this was their noise. They weren't too fussy about people's dustbins, speed was everything to those rubbish men and they often left a few lids rolling about in the road. People were always complaining.

It went quiet after a minute; then he heard car engines, and what sounded like motor bikes roaring off. The Frog music was starting up again but feebly, as though only half the electricity was coming through.

'Give us our money back,' someone shouted as the screen grew darker and darker, turning the monster to a little green blob on Paddington Station. People started to laugh and stamp, but Henry was still listening to what was going on outside. The dustbin lids had stopped clanging and the various engine noises had stopped too. Just as the projector packed in completely he heard a siren, starting far away and coming nearer.

He decided to go and have a look. Perhaps there'd been an accident on Jubilee Road. A multi-vehicle pile-up would probably be more interesting than staying here, even if they did mend the machinery. But Fatso with the Glasses was stationed at the back with his arms neatly folded, inspecting the audience row by row, and to get out Henry would have to walk right past him. He burrowed down in his seat again, wishing he had a black moustache and a false nose.

The manager stood there till the lights went on for the intermission and the ice cream lady. The thriller might be better than The Frog but Henry didn't dare stay any longer. It was already half past eight and his mother would go round to Nev's at nine o'clock. That was his deadline.

She was all mixed up, Mum was. It was all right if she was hours late, but Henry had to stick to the rules.

Outside it was chucking it down and the streets were deserted. There were no ambulances around, and no police cars, and if there had been some kind of accident the rain must have washed it all away. The heavens had really opened now and he was going to have to walk home. You couldn't go three stops on a bus with 3p. He shouldn't have bought that chocolate.

He trudged off miserably down Jubilee Road with the cold rain dripping from his ear lobes. He had that sinking feeling. He knew, even before he got there, that the leg would have gone, and as he crossed over to Alice Modes' dustbins his worst suspicions were confirmed. Nothing was as he'd left it.

The three bins were there all right but one was now lying on its side, flattened as if a steamroller had gone over it. The other two were much fuller than before, as though someone had been stuffing extra rubbish in, and he could see a great bundle of wire coat-hangers sticking out of a box.

Henry wasn't bothering tonight – he'd got coat-hangers anyway. It was the leg he wanted. He could have kicked himself. He'd exchanged that leg for two hours' boredom in which a giant frog had pulverized the entire Royal Family. He should have taken it while he had the chance.

Then he saw a pink foot sticking out from under a parked car. After the recent blood-bath in Westminster Abbey his heart flipped over and his head swam about. He'd definitely heard sirens while he was in the Essoldo; they could well have been ambulances and this foot might belong to –

Don't be *ridiculous*, he told himself sternly and marching straight across the road he bent down and grabbed. The foot was cold, plastic and hard. It had never been alive. He pulled the whole leg out and hugged it. Some maniac must have come roaring down here in the wet and skidded into Alice

Modes' dustbins, scattering rubbish all over the road. Some-one else must have helpfully stuffed it all back again. All except the leg. Lucky old Henry.

He wanted to examine it at once, under the street light. Then he thought of his mother, anxiously hammering on Nev's front door. If Mrs Hodgkinson reported that she'd not seen Henry all night Mrs Hooper might panic, and he didn't want that, not now he'd got the leg and the evening had turned out better than he'd expected. Happiness was a funny thing.

He walked springily down the main road towards the turn-off that led to the Springfield Executive Development. It was such a wet night that there was no one left in town to look at him anyway, no one to snigger at the shapely pink foot with its red toe-nails, sticking out jauntily from under one arm.

But somebody else had spotted that leg. As he went past the entrance to Egypt Street, a little side-road that led to the canal, he collided with a silent hairy figure all muffled up in a trailing plastic mac. It was Desperate Dan minus carrier bags. What on earth was he doing here? Why wasn't he at home, going through his pickings?

The old man lurched up to Henry and made a peculiar hissing noise. That was another of Eunice Snell's theories, that he was a bit weak in the head and probably stone deaf too. Otherwise, why didn't he talk in proper sentences like normal human beings?

There was nothing much wrong with Danny Crompton's head. People with addled brains didn't make a small fortune from scrap-metal and he could certainly talk when he had to. He could say 'cup of tea' and 'Give us a quid for a packet of fags' anyway; it was that which had got Father Snell into trouble with hawk-eyed Eunice. Danny simply talked when he had to, and not otherwise. It seemed reasonable enough to Henry.

But the way the man kept poking and prodding at the leg unnerved him. There were no street lights in Egypt Street, and the rain was still bucketing down, and sending cold trickles down his neck. He wanted to get home now and he wasn't going to give up his find. He was half a head taller

than Desperate Dan, and a lot heavier. 'Gedoff, Danny,' he said, giving him a push.

But the old man wouldn't go away; he was feverishly trying to yank the leg out from under Henry's arm. He'd been drinking; the boy could smell it now. That was it, he'd been in the Bay Horse and had one too many.

'I said *Gedoff!*' Henry repeated, still rather frightened but bolder now he'd realized Danny was simply tipsy. Eventually he gave him a great big shove, tightened his grip on the leg, and pelted off down Willow Way. He knew a short cut through there, along an alley, and it would get him on to the estate quicker than going along the main road.

He collided with his mother on the front step of Fir Grove. She was opening an old red umbrella and pulling her coat on.

'Hello, love,' she said. 'I was just going to Nev's. You're *late*. I was starting to worry.'

It was dark in the porch because the light socket was broken. She didn't see the leg and Henry managed to drop it into the old umbrella stand on his way into the hall. It could wait there while he had something to eat. It was hours since his fish and chips, and he was hollow.

It was only later, when he bit into his double-bacon-and-egg sandwich, that he realized why old Danny Crompton might have been pestering him. He'd only got a war-issue wooden leg after all. Perhaps he was fed up of it.

7

His mother was bursting to tell him something, her mouth was open and she'd got that glassy look. She wasn't listening to a word he said. It was only about Miss Bingham and the Beast Improvement Course, but he gave up after a few minutes and concentrated on eating.

'I've got a job, love,' she said triumphantly. 'With the *Examiner. And* I've got a lodger. That's what kept me so long at your gran's.'

The word 'lodger' roused Henry's darkest suspicions. Mum's lodgers hadn't been a success in the past, either they'd not paid the rent or else they'd pinched things. The last one had smoked in bed and set fire to the curtains. Henry was against lodgers.

'Now don't pull a face, it's someone we know.'

'Who?'

'It's Noreen.'

'Who's Noreen?'

'You know, Uncle Jack's girl. *Cousin* Noreen.'

'Oh, *her.*' Henry lost interest immediately. It was years since he'd seen Cousin Noreen. She was a fat little girl with ginger plaits who was always going to the toilet at parties.

'Why's she coming here?' he said moodily.

'Well, your uncle's retiring and they've bought a house near Harrogate, but Noreen's just started an art course at the Poly, and she wants to go on with it.'

'Which room is she having?' He might as well know, it was obviously all settled.

Mrs Hooper paused. He wasn't going to like this.

'I'm giving her the other attic.'

'Oh Mum, *why*?' The third floor was Henry's little kingdom; he dreamed his dreams up there, and he didn't want Cousin Noreen barging in, and interfering.

'She paints, and she makes sculptures and things. She needs *space*. Now don't be awkward, Henry.'

'Well, it'll be a mess,' he grumbled.

'That's funny, coming from you. Listen, chick, we need the cash and Noreen's perfect. Better the devil you know than the devil you don't. Come on, it's bedtime. We'll clear it all out at the weekend.'

He liked the 'we'; he'd be the person humping all the junk around, he was stronger than his mother. Anyway, she was too easily distracted; she'd end up sitting on the floor with a mug of tea and a fag, giggling over old photographs. He could just see it.

Cash. Everything boiled down to cash in the end. They didn't need a lodger at Fir Grove, they needed Dad back.

'Why haven't we ever got any money?' Henry said suddenly. Mrs Hooper jumped. This was his 'dangerous' voice; he wasn't easily fobbed off in this mood.

'What d'you mean, chick? We've got a roof over our heads, haven't we, and this great big house, and clothes to wear . . .'

She shouldn't have mentioned the clothes.

'Yes, and just look at them. I lost three buttons off that shirt this morning during register; I'm going to have to *slim*, Mum. Everyone laughed too. I look a right nit in that uniform. We're *poor*, that's what we are, we're *poor*.'

She hesitated. 'Well, the money side takes a long time, Henry, when . . . when people, you know . . . split up, and . . .'

'But isn't there this money Dad's supposed to pay you, this maintenance? Isn't it like the family allowance or something? Anything'd help.' He needed a replacement for his Raleigh Winner, not to mention a purple shirt with size 14 collar.

'Maintenance comes after the divorce settlement, Henry,' his mother said, in a voice that was trying to stay calm but not quite succeeding. She wouldn't look him in the eyes any more either. 'Nothing's really settled yet, and your dad's not always easy to get hold of. That's why cash is short.'

If he asked any more questions she was going to burst into

tears and Henry wouldn't be able to stand that. He gave her a secret, sideways look; her face was white and tight, like paper stretched over a frame. He loved his dad but he loved Mum too, and she was the one who'd been walked out on and left. He decided to go to bed, out of the way.

He tried to get upstairs inconspicuously, with his leg, but his mother saw it.

'What on earth do you want that for, Henry?' she said. It was the left leg of a female fashion dummy, all jagged round the top where someone had wrenched it from its plastic socket.

'I don't really know,' he muttered. He felt stupid when he saw his mother's face. She was standing in the dingy hallway looking from him to the leg with disbelief. He was definitely getting worse. For the first time it occurred to Ivy Hooper that her son might be slightly mad. His last school report had been good though – 'an excellent head for figures' the maths teacher had written. He got that from his dad of course, together with his wandering habits.

Upstairs Henry propped the leg in a corner of the attic and pulled his pyjamas on. His purple horrors were neatly laid out on a chair again, all ready for the next morning, but the tight buttonless shirt had been replaced by a brand new one.

He picked it up and started to remove all the pins. His mother was infuriating but she cared about him, deep down. All the time he'd been going on about the buttons popping off, this shirt had been up here, waiting for him. Henry wished now that he'd not made such a fuss about the perishing uniform. There was no money for shirts.

Before getting into his mattress he went into the front attic. They were going to have a field day at the weekend, it was piled high on all sides with bulging cardboard boxes. Nothing interesting though; Henry had been through it all carefully years ago.

From the window he could see right down the weedy drive to the front gate. In the road there was an ugly concrete street light; it silhouetted their rotten fence against the rainy sky and shone down on the neat standard roses in Snells' front garden. Two figures stood under it in the pouring rain. One was nothing more than a blackish blur with a pink blob for a face, but there was something rather familiar about its companion. It was short and hairy and it wore a long plastic mac.

He watched them for a minute as they stood in the ring of orange lamplight, staring up at Fir Grove. Then he saw them separate and disappear into the gloom. The big black one mounted a motor cycle and roared off, leaving the old man to hobble away through the estate on his wooden leg.

It made Henry feel rather nervous, and he wondered if he ought to go down to tell his mother. But then he had second thoughts. If she knew Danny Crompton had been pestering him in Jubilee Road she'd want to know all the details. Then she'd find out about his little trip to *The Frog That Ate London*. He'd better keep quiet for the moment; Desperate Dan did hang about the estate anyway, and he probably had all kinds of funny drinking companions, down at the Bay Horse.

The alarm clock rang at six-fifteen next morning. Henry sat up with a jolt and stared round. In the light of common day the shiny pink leg looked a bit silly. And Henry *felt* silly. He got up, scrambled into his clothes, and chucked it in his wardrobe. It could stay there till he decided what to do with it. He might get a brainwave during school, or he might end up selling it to Desperate Dan. The old man definitely fancied it. Perhaps he didn't want a leg transplant after all; perhaps he'd got the rest of the body tucked away in his house in Egypt Street. A complete fashion dummy must be worth something.

The morning was grey and drizzly and Henry skidded a couple of times as he pedalled along the towpath. This was another thing he'd have to keep from his mother – he couldn't swim and she'd told him not to go near the canal. Getting away like this before school wasn't going to be so easy when Cousin Noreen was on the other side of the attic wall. She might spy on him.

His enthusiasm for the hedgehog business was definitely waning. He didn't really trust Graham Snell to keep his mouth shut for one thing, and besides, he ought to find out what the man was paying. He might phone this evening while his mother was watching television.

The local hedgehog community must have had an all-night party because Henry found three in quick succession. He could hardly believe it. There was a fourth, but it was too squashed to be much good to the mad scientist. He'd brought an old pair of rubber gloves this time because he really didn't like touching them. When he scooped the poor things up he closed his eyes tight.

'The need for money sometimes makes people do funny things.' Henry spelled the sentence out to himself as he rode home. It was quite stylish for him; it'd certainly do for the essay on 'My Ambition'. Only another page and three quarters to go and he'd have finished.

School was depressing. It was only the second day and he already felt like a long holiday. On the bus Graham Snell had started hinting that he'd need some more ceiling tiles if he was going to co-operate about the freezer. It was blackmail.

'Look,' Henry said fiercely, 'we've made an agreement and you've got to stick to it. Shove off anyway, I'm trying to finish my homework.' It wasn't so easy either, the bus jogged and jolted and he was using Nev Hodgkinson's back to lean on.

There hadn't been time before, not with breakfast and Mum's plans for the attic, and squeezing into his shorts. So 'My Ambition' came to an abrupt end as the bus stopped at the end of Bell Street. It was like a rocket, brilliant to start with then fizzling out to nothing. Henry was a whizz kid at sums, but his English was definitely patchy.

In the form room all anyone could talk about was the sponsored cycle ride and the new band; in fact Olivia was already scraping away on her violin when Graham, Nev and Henry walked in. It was a piece called 'Fairy Dance' and it sounded terrible, as if thousands of fairies were being slowly crushed to death.

The minute Miss Bingham appeared she told Olivia to put it away. 'We don't need your instruments till next Monday, dear,' she murmured, honey sweet. 'And it's Wednesday today. Unless I've got the date wrong.'

'But, Miss Bingham, I only –'

'Put it *away*, dear,' the teacher cooed, but in rather a different voice.

Olivia was furious. She'd planned to treat everyone to 'Goblin Revels' too, now that was really difficult.

Henry watched the scene with satisfaction. Good old Goldilocks. That was the way to deal with show-offs like Olivia Onions. Though when he thought of his scrappy essay he quaked rather. What might she say about that? There was a sharp little tongue under all that glamour.

At break everyone got their pink sponsor forms out and compared notes. The Oakdene people had obviously walked all round Beeswood yesterday afternoon, getting people they knew to sign on, and now they were totting all the figures up, and bragging. It didn't seem to matter what they were raising money *for*, they'd just got to raise more of it than anyone else.

Grandad Clegg's job down Darnley Pit had ruined his lungs and he'd died. Henry could just remember all the flowers, after the funeral. Gran had wept. Jonathan Pargetter and Mavis Bramley were having an argument now, about who'd got most sponsors; they'd be fighting in a minute. It might embarrass them if Henry told them about his grandad. Perhaps it would stop them.

But he said nothing in the end. He just went away on his own to have a long private think.

If anybody in Class Six deserved to go on that sponsored cycle ride for the Miners' Home it was him, and if his mother couldn't buy him a new bike he'd just have to get one himself. He'd been hoarding his junk for long enough anyway, and it was time to liquidize his assets. He would have to sell something.

8

When they got off the bus that afternoon he saw Desperate Dan lolling in a doorway. He was clutching his carrier bags and he seemed no different from usual; in fact he wasn't even looking at them. But he still followed the three boys home, down Jubilee Road, along Willow Way and out on to the estate.

'He's after us,' Graham Snell said, quickening his pace. 'He stinks too, and those clothes must be crawling. I'm telling my mother about this.'

'Oh, give over,' Nev said gruffly. 'You're neurotic, you are. Why can't you just leave him alone? It's a free country, he's not doing us any harm.'

'But he's *following* us.'

'No he's not,' said Henry, knowing perfectly well that he was. But he'd got to put Graham off the scent. He didn't want them to get into conversation with Danny Crompton, in case he asked about the leg. He felt silly enough already. It was twenty-four hours since he'd rescued it from under that car, and he was beginning to wonder why he'd had such a craze for it. It could become an embarrassment.

Desperate Dan followed them on the Thursday night too. 'Clear off!' Graham Snell shouted, and he did, this time. He scuttled off towards Egypt Street with his carrier bags like an eighty-year-old bunny rabbit; he was quite a sharp mover considering his wooden leg. But he wasn't there on the Friday. Henry wondered whether Mrs Snell had gone into battle and phoned the police.

The answer was much nearer home. As he trudged up the jungly drive of Fir Grove, swinging his school bag, a whiskery figure popped out from behind a blackened holly bush and made a grab for him. ' 'Ere,' it said fiercely. 'Come on.'

Henry shook the arm off violently. He wasn't afraid of Danny Crompton, not when he was only inches away from his own front door, and the old man was sober this time. 'Clear off!' he yelled. If his mother was at home she'd probably hear him and come out. If she didn't he'd shout 'Dad, *Dad!*' That'd do the trick.

'Well come on then, give it us, will you?' He meant the leg.

'All right, but I want five pounds for it,' said Henry, quick as a flash. That should settle him. But it didn't. A puzzled, faraway look had come into the old man's eyes and he tugged at his grizzled beard, and pulled his mouth about.

'Three,' he said slowly. 'Three quid you can have. Come on, sonny, it's worth that. Do an old man a favour.' His tone was wheedling now, and he was feeling in his pockets for the money.

Henry couldn't believe it. Three pounds for a second-hand left leg from Alice Modes' dustbins? He stood open-mouthed by the holly bush and watched as the dirty pound notes were unrolled, counted, and shoved under his nose. Then he said 'No' quite firmly, and pushed the wrinkled old hand away. Something was up, and he wasn't parting with that leg. Not yet anyway. The minute he got inside he was going up to his room to give it a microscopic examination.

When he refused, Desperate Dan turned nasty. He scrunched his money up again, then went for Henry with both hands. 'Give it us, will you?' he hissed, through stained broken teeth. 'I'm offering you good money, aren't I? Now come on, laddie.'

There was a brown bottle sticking out of his pocket. What if he smashed the top off and went for Henry with a piece of broken glass? There were reports of street fights every week in the *Darnley Examiner*. People really got mangled sometimes, and ended up in the Borough General Hospital with stitches and blood transfusions.

He was frightened now. Danny's filthy fingernails were digging into his neck and his one foot was treading on Henry's toes. It hurt too, he'd got a big heavy boot on. 'Get *off*, Danny,' he shouted desperately, pushing at him and trying to unstick those clinging, grasping hands. But the old man's eyes had a wild hungry look in them; he was wheezing and spitting and his words had become confused and blurred. But Henry had got the message. He wasn't leaving without that leg. *See?*

He was saved by the noisy arrival of an old van. It shot through the gates and up the drive at lightning speed, and skidded to a halt by the holly bush. 'Is this Hoopers', mate?' a voice said. 'Is this Fir Grove?' The face peering through the driver's window was pasty, young and flat. The man had a large gold ring dangling from one ear-lobe, and hair like tangled yellow string. But his smile was big and friendly.

'Ye-es, yes it's Hoopers',' Henry stammered. 'I'm having a bit of trouble actually.'

The van was daubed with rainbow stripes and the word 'Lollocks' was written across them in wiggly pink letters. On the two rear doors someone had painted a lot of Ban-the-Bomb badges, all linked together to make patterns. It was quite clever.

The man looked at the bulky scared-faced boy in the tight little shorts, then at Desperate Dan. He'd already loosened his grip on Henry's neck; he was chunnering to himself now, and shuffling his feet nervously. The minute the van door opened he was off, down the drive and round the corner, leaving a stale whisky smell by the holly bush, and a shaking Henry.

'Hop in,' said the man with the hair. 'I'm Fred Holt. Noreen's my girl, I've brought her small stuff. Giving you trouble, was he? You should put a padlock on those gates, mate.'

'Oh, he's always hanging around,' Henry said vaguely, weak at the knees with relief but reluctant to go into details. He was determined to get upstairs to look at his leg, and he didn't want to get trapped into long explanations.

His mother was down at Tesco's doing the weekend shopping, so he helped Fred to lug three tea-chests into the hall. They were full of books and weighed a ton. If this was the small stuff what was the big stuff like? Those stairs might collapse on Sunday, when Noreen planned to move in. They'd got rampaging woodworm.

He quite liked Fred Holt though. If this was his cousin's boyfriend she had good taste, though if he came to see her often there'd be trouble from Mrs Snell. She wouldn't approve of the clanking rainbow-coloured van, or the skin-tight leather pants, and she certainly wouldn't like all his badges, or the studs that spelt 'Peace' all over the back of his jacket. She didn't understand people like that, and they frightened her.

'Do you ban the bomb then?' Henry said curiously, as Fred climbed back into his van. 'Do you go on marches?'

'Now and again,' said Fred, 'when I've not got a gig.'

'What's a gig?'

'It's a band job. The Lollocks is a pop group; I'm the drummer. Look, I'm late. See you, mate,' and he rattled off down the drive.

It sounded quite promising. If Miss Bingham's idea for the band came to anything Henry just might ask him about playing that washboard with thimbles.

The minute he got upstairs he shut his door and examined the leg minutely, but he gave up in the end. It was a perfectly ordinary leg from a shop dummy. He measured it carefully with an old steel tape and found it was 31½ inches long. It was hollow too, and because of the hole in the top you could see right into it. Henry was a boy who left no stone unturned, and he got a torch and shone the beam inside.

It looked empty and it *was* empty. He'd already turned it upside down and shaken it half a dozen times, but nothing had fallen out except a bit of grit. Now he gave it one last violent shake for luck. Nothing, not even dust and feathers. Not even Eunice Snell could have got anything out of that leg, not even with her special Hoover attachment for getting into corners.

He threw it on to his mattress and viewed it from a distance, pink and whole. Perhaps the foot was the clue, perhaps he should get a saw and cut it off. There might be something stuck in the ankle joint.

'Sleep on it, Henry.' The one bit of really good advice his father had given him floated into his mind as he stood there staring at his leg. There may well be a very simple answer to this, something so obvious he hadn't even considered it.

Sawing that leg in half was the last act of a desperate man, and he wasn't *that* desperate. The chances were that old Danny Crompton was just being funny about it – he was a funny man.

For the rest of the day Henry made plans. The leg was his biggest worry, with this curious hold it had over Desperate Dan, but there were other things too, not worries so much as untied ends.

Henry had a tidy mind, and he was practical. He'd got a lot of schemes in hand, but none of them had come to anything. It was time to get himself organized while he had the chance. Cousin Noreen was arriving on Sunday and life wasn't going to be so free and easy after that. She might cramp his style.

While his mother was watching *Look North* he crept downstairs and phoned the Poly, but they told him Dr Barraclough wasn't available till next week. That was blow number one. Blow number two was Eunice Snell's complete failure as a mother. She was thinner than ever and completely terrorized by Big Daddy. No matter how cunning Henry was at feeding time he always got to the grub first, and Eunice just watched him eat it, shivering away in the furthest corner of the cage.

His suspicions of these two were growing by the minute, strengthened by his suspicions about Nev Hodgkinson. Nev was always full of beans but he was distinctly slippery. Well, he'd be getting a caller tomorrow.

Henry sat glumly on his mattress watching Big Daddy stuff himself and reading the notice board that hung over his bookshelf. It was covered with scraps of paper, including a few bits of poetry he'd written in the last couple of days, since the Kelly Kitchen leaflet had arrived wrapped up in the *Star*.

Give your mum a treat, make her things to eat,
Get in the kitchen and . . .

He'd not been able to make up an ending for that one; perhaps the next was a bit better:

Your cooking goes without a hitch in
A nice new apron and a Kelly Kitchen.

Well the rhyme was quite clever, but somehow it didn't have the prize-winning ring to it.

The truth was that Henry couldn't write poetry to save his life, and his efforts to win a dream kitchen were pathetic. Anyway, Mavis Bramley was doing the competition too, and she was very good. Her father was an English teacher at the Comp and her essay on 'My Ambition' had been six and a half pages long. That was another blow.

After some thought Henry climbed on to his chest of drawers and got something down from the top of his wardrobe. It was an old wooden tool-box painted black, and there was a neat gummed label on the lid, 'My Most Precious Possessions'.

He laid them all out on the mattress. There was a tobacco-tin full of old coins, a broken air rifle he'd bought at a jumble sale and a framed photo of his dad. Henry was on it too, and his mother. Someone had taken it for them three years ago, at Grange-over-Sands. He'd put it away when Dad walked out; he didn't like looking at it any more. That picture stood for something simple and happy, something that had ended last Christmas and would never come back. Unless his father suddenly came breezing up the path one day. And was that likely, now Sheila Howarth had got her clutches on him?

There was also a rusty old tin. It looked nothing much but it was worth more than money could buy; it was Grandad Clegg's snap-box, from down the mine. He used to take bread and cheese down in that.

Well he certainly wasn't selling the tin, or the air gun, and the coins couldn't be worth much. The obvious thing was the gold watch, wrapped up at the bottom in a bit of cloth. It *was* gold; Henry had polished it up and found the special marks on it. He couldn't believe his luck when he'd come across that watch, at the bottom of an old biscuit-tin on Chorley Street dump, under a lot of nuts and bolts. He'd beaten Danny Crompton to it that time.

Even if the works were all gunged up the gold case must be worth something. They would probably weigh it and work out the value that way. Henry had contacts in Jubilee Road, and he knew exactly where to go. But he was going to clean it up again first.

He could do that in bed. Now he'd organized his life he felt slightly more cheerful, and cheerfulness always made him hungry. He decided to go downstairs and ask his mother for a bacon sandwich and if he could watch telly for a bit. At least she'd been to Tesco's. Friday was the only night he was really sure of getting enough to eat.

9

Next day was Saturday. He was up early again but he didn't go hedgehog-hunting. It was cold and there was a lot to do. Anyway, he wasn't going to get any more until he'd agreed on a price with the mad scientist and there were already four of the things, snugly hidden under the sprouts in Eunice Snell's freezer. If he got 50p a head that'd be two pounds, and he might get more.

Fifty pence a head reminded him of Call Number One. He was supposed to be getting that for the gerbil babies, but his hopes were fading. The best he could hope for was to persuade Nev Hodgkinson to give him his money back. It was embarrassing because Nev was a friend, but he was determined to try.

Just after eight o'clock he was knocking on the battered front door with his gerbil cage under his arm. Desperate Dan had been stationed outside the gates of Fir Grove and it had startled Henry. He was in a positive cheerful mood this morning, and his mind wasn't on the leg, so when the familiar hairy face swam into view he'd acted without thinking. He hadn't done anything; he'd just said 'Look, Danny, I don't know what you're after but I'm fed up. That man saw you yesterday, and my mum knows you're around. If you don't lay off the police'll be after you. *Now get lost!*'

And it did the trick. At the word 'police' the old man scuttled off towards the main road without another word. Somehow Henry felt mean afterwards; that kind of talk reminded him of Eunice Snell. But he couldn't just ignore Danny Crompton. It made him think about that leg though; Desperate Dan was *obsessed*.

He knocked three times on Hodgkinsons' front door but it was all very quiet. The family had a lie-in on Saturdays. Eventually Nev's mother opened an upstairs window and shoved her head out. She was wearing a pink flowered dressing-gown and rollers. 'Oh, it's you, Henry. It's a bit early, isn't it? What do you want?'

'Can I speak to Nev, please. It's about these gerbils.'

He regretted the last bit afterwards. Mrs Hodgkinson went away, came back, and said Nev was still fast asleep and could he call later. But he wasn't asleep; Henry had seen a little face peeping through a slit in the curtains. He shouldn't have said what he wanted, and he should have left the gerbil cage hidden behind the fence.

'All right, I'll come back,' he shouted, and he set off towards Jubilee Road. It'd take him twenty minutes to walk into town and by then it'd be half past eight and they'd have opened up the Covered Market.

He got there just as the parish church clock was striking. The old market was a tempting place, especially when you were an early customer like Henry. It was full of interesting smells and men whistling and shouting, and delivery-boys cycling about with baskets full of chops and sausages. There was always plenty of fascinating rubbish too, no matter what time of day it was. But he wasn't scavenging today. He walked straight up the central aisle into the pet store at the far end, and dumped his gerbils on the counter.

He was the only customer in the shop so the jowly-looking man behind the till gave him his full attention. He was fat and his cheeks wobbled when he talked. Perhaps he kept bulldogs; people were supposed to grow like their pets after a while. 'Can I help you, son?' he said pleasantly.

Henry explained that he wanted to sell his gerbils. 'They're supposed to be having babies,' he explained, 'and I was going to sell those. But, well, there's nothing doing, and I've been waiting for weeks.'

The man thrust his great jowls right up to the cage. Big Daddy squeaked and Eunice Snell hid in the straw. 'Well *she* looks ready to produce,' he said admiringly. 'What a whopper. I'd hang on to her if I were you.'

'No,' said Henry. 'That's the male. It's the thin one that's pregnant. Well that's what Nev said.'

'Mind if I look?'

'N-no,' faltered Henry, watching a great red hand disappear into the wire cage. One by one the gerbils were scooped up, turned over, inspected, and dropped back.

The man snapped the little door shut and looked at Henry rather sorrowfully. 'How long did you say you'd been waiting?' he said.

'Weeks.'

'Well don't wait any longer, son, they're both males. You've been done.'

I knew it, thought Henry. All that money, all that cleaning out, all that careful feeding for nothing. *Both males*, and just look at them. One needed to go on a crash diet, the other was in the middle of a nervous breakdown. He didn't want them any more.

'Will you buy them off me?' he said tentatively. 'I don't want much for them, and they're a real mess at home. I only got them for the babies.'

The man with the jowls looked thoughtful. There was something a bit comical about the hopeful freckled face, but something sad too. There was a kind of longing in the boy's eyes. He looked so crestfallen that Old Bulldog didn't know what to do for a minute. Then three people came into the shop at once and stood in a line, waiting to be served.

'Look, son,' he said quickly. 'I really can't take them, I'm overrun with gerbils at the moment, there's . . . well there's a glut. But I'll tell you what I'll do. Put the little one in this,' and he produced a small rusty cage from under the counter. 'It's old but it's escape-proof. He'll do better in there; he's not thriving. Keep them for another six weeks and then bring them back if you want to. I'll buy them then; I always get a lot in for Christmas.'

Like turkeys, Henry thought gloomily, plodding back through the Covered Market. Like sherry. The man had been very reasonable but the place for those gerbils was down Nev Hodgkinson's neck. He'd do it as well, given half the chance. Meanwhile he was rechristening them The Two Ronnies.

He had another go at Nev as he walked home through the estate. The Hodgkinsons had all surfaced now; Art's skinny legs were sticking out from under a three-wheeled Morris Minor in the garden and the twins were sitting inside it, fighting over the steering wheel. Henry didn't even have time to knock on the door. 'He's not in,' Sandra yelled. 'He's gone to our Marian's with me dad.'

Our Marian was a married cousin in Leeds. Sandra's story may or may not be true but the jungle drums had been beating while Henry was at the market and Nev was obviously planning to lie low for the whole weekend.

Henry hung around for a few minutes then gave the gatepost a kick and went home. Whichever way you looked at it he'd been swindled.

10

Fir Grove was as quiet as the grave because Mrs Hooper had been having a lie-in too. She started her new job on Monday and she said she needed her beauty sleep before tackling the front attic. Henry went up to his room, rearranged his shelves to take the new cage, gave Little Ronnie a bite to eat and went straight out again. He wasn't feeding Big Ronnie – he'd already eaten enough for three today. It was disgusting.

He'd cleaned up his pocket-watch with metal polish and an old duster, and it looked quite nice. It was a proper gentleman's 'hunter' and he surely couldn't get less than ten pounds for it, even though it didn't work. It felt like a smooth sea pebble down in his jeans pocket and he kept feeling it as he walked along. Half of him didn't want to part with it, but that was stupid. You didn't make money by hanging on to things, and it *was* gold. Mr Schofield would give him a good price for it; he was always fair with Henry, and Grandad Clegg had been his best friend. They used to go bowling together.

But Henry had a shock when he got to the shop. The little watchmenders-cum-jewellers tucked away down an alley between Jubilee Road and Edith Street was all boarded up, and there was a cardboard box on the pavement full of broken glass.

A notice on the boards said 'Business As Usual' and he could see a light inside. Henry pushed the door open and went in. Mr Schofield was sitting behind his counter mending something, but the shop felt different somehow. None of the clocks and watches were ticking. Mr Schofield usually went round at twelve o'clock Greenwich Mean Time rewinding and resetting; Henry had helped him once. But all the clocks had stopped today and the silence was uncanny. It was like being in a room full of corpses.

'Hello, Henry,' the old man said at last. 'We've been done again, son. First they did the electric shop next door, then they did me. I wish they'd come and take all that rubbish away from outside, I just can't lift it.' Then he lapsed into silence again and put a thick black eyeglass into position to examine a wrist-watch. Henry had always fancied that eyeglass. When he was little he used to watch Mr Schofield fiddle with it, half expecting it to disappear through a little hole in his face.

He wasn't getting anywhere with the repair though; both his hands were shaking and his voice had a queer, strangled feel about it.

'Was it on Tuesday?' Henry said suddenly, little bells starting to ring in his head.

'That's right, son. Been in the *Examiner* has it? They're quick.'

'No,' Henry explained cautiously. 'Only I was at the pictures, and I heard the sirens. Never thought it was you though. Did they take much?'

The old man paused. 'Ne'er . . . usual stuff, you know. Clocks and watches, digital mainly, that's the stuff they go for these days. They were obviously a bunch of cowboys – they dropped half the stuff in the main road. Someone was driving an old van, and crashed it.'

'Outside the dress shop?'

'That's right. How did you –'

'I saw the bins,' said Henry. 'So they caught them then?'

There was another lengthy silence. The old man's hands were shaking so much he'd let the wrist-watch fall on to the counter and he sat nodding his head over it. 'No, not yet. Unbelievable isn't it? An old van and a couple of clapped-out motor bikes, and they let them get away. They'll catch them though, they were just cowboys,' he repeated.

Henry was watching the old man carefully. There was something else, something he'd not been told. Jewellers were always having break-ins; it was 'part of the trade' according to Mr Schofield. What on earth could have happened on Tuesday night?

'Mr Schofield,' he began, feeling for his gold watch. Then he stopped. The eyeglass had fallen out and was rolling about on the floor. It was when the old watchmender bent down to pick it up that his wrinkled face moved into the light, and Henry saw that he was crying.

A pang shot through him and his carefully prepared speech about selling the hunter died on his lips. It was awful, an old man like this weeping over a few cheap watches; he couldn't bear it. Mum had cried once, just once in front of Henry, when Dad had walked out and moved in with Sheila Howarth. It had been a terrible night. This was bringing it all back.

'Not feeling too good this morning, Henry,' Mr Schofield got out at last, in a tight embarrassed voice. 'It's the shock, son, they've done it to me once too often. I think I'll phone the wife and go home. There's not much doing this morning anyway.'

Henry walked back thoughtfully along Jubilee Road with the gold watch still buried in his pocket. Mr Schofield obviously wasn't well; his face had looked all grey and papery, like Grandad Clegg's before he'd died. But if it was only *watches* why had he been so upset? And why was there a 'substantial reward' offered to anyone giving useful information? He didn't usually do that after a break-in. But the notice was there, under the 'Open' sign, in his own handwriting.

Henry could always go after that, but it was a pity he'd not slipped out of the Regal when he'd first heard the sirens; he might have seen something then.

Making money wasn't nearly so easy as some people made out, Henry had decided, turning in at the rusty old gates of Fir Grove. The hedgehogs were unreliable, the gerbils were non-starters, and to win competitions you had to be some kind of genius. If you grew up and became an honest shopkeeper like Mr Schofield, you got robbed. He felt really depressed now, depressed about the old man's worries, depressed about his own.

His mother was in the bath when he got home, singing tunelessly in time with the radio. Henry wasn't really very musical but Ivy Hooper was tone-deaf. The horrible noise cheered him up somehow, it was a prelude to more breakfast and their attack on the front attic. It was going to take all day to clear that room out, and Henry definitely needed something to take his mind off his troubles.

11

Noreen arrived late in the afternoon, only minutes after Henry had lugged the last box of rubbish down the attic stairs and shoved it behind the curtains on the lower landing. He'd been trotting up and down all day and he was knackered.

'This is Noreen,' Mum announced, fresh as a daisy. It was all right for her, she'd got through two packets of fags and a gallon of tea since they'd started, not to mention all the old souvenirs.

His long-lost cousin was a bit of a shock. She was very tall, with a wild look in her eyes, and she was all black and white. When she came through the attic doorway it was like watching an old photograph spring suddenly into life.

'Are you a punk?' said Henry, before he could stop himself. Well she did look extraordinary.

'Henry,' Mrs Hooper said sharply, looking away in embarrassment. It wasn't a very good start. But he just couldn't take his eyes off her.

It must have taken her hours to get dressed and made up. She wore black and white striped clown pants, baggy, with frills, and an oversized man's shirt. One shoe was white, the other black, and there were clinking chains wound round her arms and legs. When she moved she sounded like a travelling amusement. Her finger nails were shiny long and black, and her face was floury white. He couldn't see much of it because she wore enormous mirror glasses, reflecting two little Henrys all agog. But her hair was her masterpiece, closely shaved at the sides but quite flat on top, and all dyed in black and white squares. You could have played draughts on it if you'd been able to reach up.

'Well *are* you?' he repeated dumbly. He was quite carried away by Noreen.

'I'm not really sure,' she said good-humouredly, removing the great moon spectacles and peering down at him. 'What is a punk anyway?'

'I don't know,' Henry said feebly. 'I just thought you might be one.'

'She's an *artist*, Henry,' Mrs Hooper said helplessly, tugging at an old flowered curtain and making a big rip even bigger. 'Oh *damn*!'

'Don't worry about those, Auntie Ivy,' Noreen said. 'I don't want any curtains. Actually, I was wondering if I could paint the room? This wallpaper's not me really.'

'Paint away,' said Mrs Hooper. 'It's been here since the year dot, and I've always hated it. If I sell up a bit of redecoration's bound to help.'

Henry was scowling at her from under furrowed brows. She always did this when other people were listening; it was as if she was too nervous to discuss it with him face to face. She knew he loved Fir Grove, but *he* knew that his days here were numbered, unless Dad came back.

So far the front attic was empty. It looked like a prison cell to Henry but Cousin Noreen adored it; she kept going on and

66

on about the big windows and the 'steady Northern light'. All she wanted, she said, was her big work table, her bookcases and her orthopaedic mattress. Her boyfriend was supposed to be delivering them any minute.

So Noreen slept on a mattress too, a very hard one. Henry was slightly reassured. At least she couldn't laugh at his sleeping arrangements, if she strayed into his attic.

Down in the drive someone was sounding a car horn. It was Fred Holt, delivering the big stuff. Noreen reached the front door just as his rainbow-coloured van was disappearing down the drive. 'That's typical,' she said crossly, reading a scrawled note pinned to a sagging stripey mattress. 'He's gone into town to collect a drum repair, and he's got to come back with the table. I'm sorry, Auntie Ivy.'

It had started raining so Mrs Hooper called over the back fence to Mr Snell. He'd escaped from Eunice to have a quiet smoke in the garden. He seemed quite willing to lend a hand and came straight round. Carrying a double mattress up the attic stairs had proved too much for Henry, even with Noreen and his mother shoving up from below. They needed another pair of arms.

Jack Snell was all right on his own but they hadn't reckoned with a visit from Eunice. She was a real nosey parker. She'd seen Fred Holt and his Lollocks van shoot out dangerously into the road and her curiosity and fears were roused at once. She sidled along the drive after her husband and up to the front door. Then she saw Noreen, giggling as they struggled with the bookcases.

She was terrified. She went straight home and sat at the kitchen table with a pot of strong tea, waiting for Mr Snell's return. When he came back she poured him out a cup, with a shaking hand. It was too much, she told him, the Hoopers were definitely getting worse. First they let the house go to rack and ruin, then the garden; now they were sheltering hippies. She wanted to move in the summer and there were to be no more excuses. Next door's goings on were an absolute disgrace.

Meanwhile, up in the attics, Noreen and Henry were having a fascinating conversation. Now he'd got used to it, her strange appearance didn't seem quite so alarming, and she looked more normal without the glasses. The white flour make-up was slowly flaking off as she wandered about exploring, and she'd got a nice face underneath.

'I'm going natural this winter,' she informed Henry. 'I'm letting this grow out,' and she lowered her head obligingly to show him a patch of bright ginger in the middle of the chessboard hair.

Henry stared, dimly remembering babyhood, sitting on his gran's lap while a stubby girl with ginger plaits rushed off to the lavatory in the middle of Postman's Knock. Time did amazing things to people.

'What do you think, Henry?' she said, waggling her head about.

'I don't really know,' he said dumbly. People didn't usually ask his opinion about anything. After a pause he added 'I like Fred's van', just for something to say. Then he asked, 'But does he really go banning the bomb?'

'Oh yes, when he's not doing a gig.'

'And do you go?'

'No. But I'm thinking about it.'

Henry was intrigued by Fred's doings; he wanted to know more. 'Does he have wire cutters?' he said. 'Does he climb into army bases and things?'

'Oh *no*, but he does worry about it all. Fred's nineteen, he's a serious person. Aren't *you* worried?'

'I . . . I don't know,' Henry stammered. He'd not really thought about bombs and the end of the world. Perhaps he ought to. At the moment though he'd got other problems – his parents' separation for a start, and all the mysteries surrounding that.

After a bit of persuasion he agreed to show Cousin Noreen round his attic. She was very impressed. She said the clutter was very 'Victorian' and the effect of his junk collection was quite electrifying. She went round poking and prodding and lifting things up saying 'I could use that' and 'Yes, I'll have that', like a dealer at an auction. Crazy things tickled her fancy, things like the bunches of wire coat-hangers and a stack of multi-coloured egg trays, and when she saw his leg sticking out of the wardrobe she pounced on it at once, her green eyes gleaming. 'Oh, I've got to have this, Henry,' she said. 'How much?'

He was bewildered, and slightly suspicious. Everyone was after that perishing leg, even the lodger. 'Well, what do you want all this stuff for?' he said cautiously. 'I don't usually sell it you see. It's . . . it's a kind of hobby.'

The truth was that nobody had ever made him an offer for it before. Who wanted a ton of wire coat-hangers and two million egg trays?

Noreen did. She was planning to enter a big local art competition and she wanted to make a 'sculpt'. She needed rubbish of all kinds in the early stages, to get her started, and Henry's attic was a little gold-mine.

He was fairly easily persuaded. She made him a very good offer for the coat-hangers and a big tin of nails, and he threw in some egg trays for free. They agreed that from now on Noreen would have first refusal on anything Henry found. But the leg was excluded.

'Oh, go on,' she wheedled, 'I could really do something with that.'

'No,' Henry said firmly, and he wouldn't budge. All he would say was that he promised to think about it. He'd not got to the bottom of that leg yet, by any means.

Before it went dark he took Cousin Noreen on a tour of the garden. Fir Grove looked quite romantic in the dusk, creeper-covered against the blue-black sky, with bats flitting over the roof. Noreen loved everything about it, the patterns in the crumbling brick, the fancy chimneys, even the rusty iron fire-escape that twisted up from the ground floor and ended just below Henry's window.

'Do you ever climb in that way?' she said.

'No. It's dangerous. I used to play on it but I fell off once; Mum should get it removed really but she never bothers. Perhaps she thinks it's propping the house up.'

'It's a lovely old place, Henry,' Noreen whispered, in a misty kind of voice. 'Don't let your mother sell it, will you?'

'I can't stop her, it's the money you see. She . . . she can't cope without Dad, she can't seem to manage things.'

'But hasn't all that been settled? When people get divorced the money usually –'

'They're not divorced,' Henry said very quietly. 'Not yet.

Mum's hoping he'll come back, I'm sure she is, but she just won't talk about it.'

It was too dark to see his face but Noreen heard his voice trembling slightly. 'I'm going to tell you something,' she said, putting a black manicured hand on his shoulder. 'But don't let on, will you?'

'What?'

'Sheila Howarth's moved out. Your dad's on his own now.'

This was certainly news to Henry, but he wasn't banking on it. She'd come creeping back again, complaining about Dad's crumpled collars and his scuffed shoes, sprucing him up. She was a sticker. 'I thought they were getting married,' he said miserably. 'It's hopeless.'

'There's always hope, Henry,' Noreen whispered.

'All *right*, so there's always *hope*,' Henry parroted peevishly. He often sounded rude when things were upsetting him. 'But Mum just won't *talk* to me about it, and that's not fair.'

'Let's sit down for a minute,' Noreen suggested, finding a rickety iron seat half-way down the garden and swishing the first autumn leaves off it. 'It's nice out here. Listen, love, it's painful for your mother, and she must feel guilty about you too. That's why she's so funny. Don't forget what it's like for her, Henry, day after day, hoping, just hoping, that he'll come back again. She thinks the world of your dad, in spite of this daft episode with Sheila Howarth.'

'How do *you* know?' Henry wasn't sure he liked all this comment about his private affairs. After all, she'd only just moved in. He knew she was right though, about how his mother felt.

'I was at Grandma Clegg's last week,' she told him, 'and your mum had a sort of outburst. She said she'd just seen Sheila Howarth crossing Yorkshire Street and felt like running her down with the scooter. She really does care, Henry, and she wants him home.'

No more than I do, he was thinking miserably. She couldn't want him back more than Henry did. Nobody could. When he thought of that stupid quarrel he hated them both for a minute. It was That Row that'd brought everything to a head, like a horrible boil, swelling and bursting and all the pus coming out.

They'd said some awful things to one another that night,

about Dad running after younger women and never staying at home, and about Mum keeping the house like a pigsty. And Henry had listened on the stairs with the tears running down his face; then Dad had walked out at two in the morning. It had been Christmas three days after.

'Come on,' Noreen said. 'It's damp on this bench and I'm getting a cold bottom. Now don't forget what I've told you, Henry. There's always hope. There *is*. So try to look on the bright side. It won't help at all if you mope around, now will it?'

'No,' Henry said obediently, following her back up the garden and in through the kitchen door. Behind those big moon glasses she reminded him of a young owl.

Ten minutes later Fred Holt came roaring back from Darnley with his drum repair and the last of Noreen's big stuff, a rickety trestle table which he manoeuvred expertly up three flights of stairs and arranged in the front attic to catch the steady Northern light. Down in the kitchen Noreen was proving to be a dab hand at spaghetti and Mrs Hooper produced a big bottle of cider, nicely chilled after a couple of hours in the front room.

Henry stayed up quite late and Fred gave him a lesson on his old washboard. He seemed quite interested in Miss Bingham's orchestra. Tapping out a simple rhythm didn't seem at all simple to Henry, and the thimbles kept falling off, but he got the hang of it in the end.

'Everyone's got music in them, Henry,' Fred said encouragingly. 'Stick with it, kid.'

But there was music and music. Graham Snell had spent the afternoon in his garage making rude noises on his grandfather's trombone. Miss Bingham was going to need ear-plugs on Monday morning.

It was a good night though. His mother laughed a lot and never once mentioned money, or selling the house, and Henry felt strangely at peace. Perhaps it was the cider, perhaps it was the arrival of Cousin Noreen. It was still early days, but having her as a lodger might turn out to be the one Hooper project that didn't fall flat on its face.

12

In the middle of the night a noise woke Henry. He sat up with a jerk, felt round, and switched on his owl lamp. It was a blue china barn owl with a light bulb stuck to its head. He'd found it one day on Chorley Road Tip, brought it home and got it working.

There were no curtains in his attic. Who needed curtains three floors up? Cousin Noreen liked the steady Northern light and Henry liked the sun. On fine days it woke him up in the morning.

He flashed a look round the room, switched the owl lamp off again and buried himself in his mattress, squirming right down and pulling the covers up over his head. He was shaking with fright. A big pink blob of a face was at the window, peering in at him.

For a few seconds he lay there rigid, his heart was thumping and his hands and face were sticky with sweat. Now he could hear a soft scuffling noise against the bricks outside. Whoever it was must be making a very quick getaway. The owl light had obviously scared him off.

Henry stayed exactly where he was for quite a long time, hidden in the mattress with a little tuft of hair sticking out. Then, when all was deathly quiet again, he decided to investigate. He didn't dare switch his light back on, and he banged into some shelves in the darkness. 'Second World War' and 'Miscellaneous' went crashing to the ground and he could hear a lot of nuts and bolts rolling across the floor.

The wall between the two attics was only thin plasterboard. Cousin Noreen had an artistic temperament and she was a very light sleeper. 'Henry?' she called out anxiously. 'Henry! What's going on? Are you all right?'

Henry wasn't all right. He was in a heap on his mattress with the owl light casting its feeble yellow ring on his sweaty frightened face. 'There was someone looking in at me,' he whispered hoarsely, 'someone spying. The noise woke me up.'

Noreen stood doubtfully in the doorway. The long granny nightie with frills at the wrists didn't really go with the amazing chequer-board hair. She was listening carefully to all he said but it was obvious that she didn't believe a word of it.

'Are you *sure*, Henry?' she said.

'I'm *positive*.' He could still see that great pink blob quite clearly, in his mind.

'But how could anyone get up here? On the outside? Come off it, he'd have to be thirty feet tall.'

'You've forgotten the fire-escape,' said Henry coldly.

But Noreen still wasn't convinced. She listened very patiently, and pondered, but in the end she drifted back to bed and advised Henry to do the same. He was quite grown up for his age and he took life seriously, which was why she liked him. But he *had* had three glasses of cider on top of all that spaghetti bolognese. He'd obviously got a bit of a hangover.

Henry couldn't get back to sleep again. After about twenty minutes he crept out of bed and went over to the window, half hoping for another glimpse of The Blob, just to show Cousin Noreen he'd not made it up.

It was never completely black through that window. Now they'd opened the motorway extension an orange haze always hung over the moors. It spoiled it really. There was a big moon tonight and he could see the Darnley Canal running away from the Rec, a shiny black ribbon that started at their back fence and ended at Spring Mill.

The mill was a ruin. It shouldn't have got like that but there was a long legal argument going on between two rich families about who owned the land it was built on. After it was closed down the Platts wanted to demolish it, to redevelop the site, and the Pollitts wanted to convert the buildings into a slipper

73

factory. They'd been arguing for three years now. It'd still be there when they were all dead, grinning at everyone with its horrible eyeless stare.

The *Examiner* reported regularly on the Platt–Pollitt dispute. One week the Pollitts sent people to put chains and padlocks all over the gates, the next the Platts came along and took them all off again. Then everyone went to court and argued about it. It was a riot.

Last summer Henry had played for hours in Spring Mill, with Nev Hodgkinson. Even with the Pollitt padlocks on you could get inside, if you were small enough. There was a hole in the wall that bordered the canal bank and you could squeeze through into the foundations. Nev reckoned you'd end up in the main cellars if you went far enough, but they never had. It was extremely dark and smelly in there.

They might have done if Mrs Hooper hadn't found out

74

where they'd been going, and stopped them. She'd really shouted at Henry. She was a miner's daughter so she'd got pit disasters on the brain. 'You'll get killed crawling round in there,' she'd yelled at him. 'Anything could happen, a wall could collapse on you or anything. Now you don't go in there again Henry. *Get it?'*

Henry hadn't. His mother was scatty about most things but she was dead serious about Spring Mill. She'd kill him if he disobeyed and Nev's dad had threatened to belt him, if he went.

At three in the morning the mill was a big empty hulk against the orangey darkness. In front the canal water glinted and gleamed. Then Henry saw something else, a wavering light that wobbled and dipped behind one of the shattered windows.

He stared hard in case it was some kind of reflection from

the lamps on the motorway, but it wasn't, and a few seconds later he saw it again, flashing in and out of the crumbling walls. Somebody was in there, poking about.

On the Monday morning he woke up very early, just as it was getting light. The hedgehog caper had somehow affected his pattern of sleep and he was wide awake at six, with nowhere to go. He pulled his clothes on rather grumpily; he'd not had nearly enough kip, not with all those interruptions on Saturday night, and he'd been late last night too because they'd all been to tea and supper with Grandma Clegg, and not left till ten. Noreen hadn't said a word about The Blob either. She obviously thought he was barmy.

Well he wasn't going hedgehog-spotting, not till he'd fixed up a deal with the mad scientist. Then a thought struck him; he did have a whole three hours before school started. What was the harm in going to have a mosey round Spring Mill? His mother surely couldn't object if he just went and *looked* at it?

When he walked down the garden to get his fairy-cycle out of the shed he noticed that the two bottom rungs of the fire-escape were broken. Henry bent down and inspected it carefully. It certainly hadn't been like that last week – he knew Fir Grove like the back of his hand, and he knew that fire-escape. He'd not had a hangover and The Blob hadn't been Desperate Dan either. Danny was a determined old geezer but he wasn't up to climbing a fire-escape in the middle of the night.

He pedalled along the canal bank quite slowly, keeping his eyes skinned for signs of defunct animal life. Well, hedgehogs weren't just confined to motorways. But there was nothing doing on the towpath and in five minutes he was leaning his bike against the outer wall of Spring Mill. The Platts had obviously been last on the scene – the huge gates hung open and a thick rusty chain was lying on the ground in two pieces. Just inside he spotted an old motor cycle. Its petrol tank was dented and there was a big oil patch underneath, but no signs of life that Henry could see.

He crept around in the huge inner yard, looking for clues. He couldn't see very much; the sheds were still securely padlocked and the rubble-filled acres of dusty asphalt were bare and silent. Grandma Clegg had been a mill girl. She said the noise in the sheds was so terrific they'd used sign language to talk to one another.

There was something sad about Spring Mill now, with its crazed windows and its broken bricks, something a bit sinister. Henry really didn't like it. It had been different fooling about with Nev last summer, but he was on his own now.

He'd turned back towards the gates when a noise made him whip round. Someone was crunching across the rubble towards him, a youth in jeans and an old denim jacket, with greasy blonde hair and a pimply pink face. He was very fleshy and he carried a blue crash helmet under one arm. It was obviously the second-hand motor bike proprietor.

He marched straight up to Henry and the look in his eyes was none too friendly. 'What are you doing in here?' he demanded in a loud, bullying voice. 'It's private property, this is.'

Henry stood his ground and stared back hard. Well, if it *was* this man wouldn't be guarding it – he was too scruffy. Ear-rings from Woolworth's, wardrobe by Oxfam. He didn't exactly look like the Securicor man, more like a dropout from Darnley Comprehensive.

'I'm-I'm looking for hedgehogs,' Henry said firmly, staring him straight in the eyes. It sounded daft but it was true, more or less.

'Well look for them somewhere else, will you, or I'll tan your backside,' the man threatened, and he made a run at Henry and chased him right through the gates.

The boy fled. He clambered back on to his fairy-cycle and made off down the towpath, wobbling so violently he nearly rode into the canal. He was too het-up to go straight back to Fir Grove and anyway it was still only quarter to seven. So he went for a walk on the Rec instead, to calm himself down.

There was an old punctured football lying between the goal-posts. Henry kicked at it, still thinking about The Blob. He'd only seen that face at the window for a split second, on Saturday night, but it had certainly been pink and fleshy. Could it have been the demon bike rider? If so, what was he after, down at Spring Mill?

He'd have to keep quiet about his early-morning excursion for the moment. His mother had forbidden him to go near the place, and Cousin Noreen thought he was suffering from midnight hallucinations, so she'd be no help. He felt depressed, and slightly bewildered. Things were hotting up but he just couldn't think what to do next, without getting into trouble.

The only good thing about his rude awakening was the discovery of a gigantic hedgehog behind one of the goal-posts. It was undeniably dead. Perhaps it had been stunned by a penalty kick from a crack centre-forward.

He had a plastic bag in his pocket and he knelt down in the grass and scooped it up. He may as well have it, now he was here.

There didn't look much wrong with the hedgehog but it had a sad, resigned sort of a face. It must simply have given up the struggle and died. Henry knew exactly how it felt.

13

After the discovery of the hedgehog the day slid steadily downhill. On the bus to school Graham Snell went on and on about his grandad's trombone, and bragged about his great long list of sponsors for the bike ride; and relations with Nev were definitely strained.

He tried to make the peace by offering Henry a couple of rabbits.

'No thanks,' said Henry, staring stonily out of the window; rabbits were big eaters and had families fast. Anyway, he was getting used to The Two Ronnies now; he'd been quite glad to hear them nibbling away in the middle of Saturday night, when The Blob's face had suddenly appeared in the window. He was more and more certain it *was* The Blob.

Miss Bingham's first band session was rather less than absolutely fabulous; in fact it was a total disaster. Mr Stannard, the area music director, a crusty old man who looked about four foot six, inspected the array of assembled 'instruments' and obviously thought he'd been conned. For a start he couldn't stand recorders, and Mavis Bramley was immediately banished to the back row, to play a triangle. Then Olivia snapped her E-string while tuning up and was unable to demonstrate 'Goblin Revels', and Nev was told off for doing aircraft imitations on Graham Snell's trombone.

Everyone was arguing about where to sit in the hall and the noise was deafening. 'My time, my time, children,' Miss Bingham twittered feebly, flashing her teeth.

Mr Stannard was more direct. 'Find something to sit on and SIT ON IT!' he bellowed. For such a small man he had a remarkably big voice.

There was no disobeying a voice like that – he was worse than The Beast. Everyone scurried about looking for an empty seat, and Henry just slumped down where he was, on Jonathan Pargetter's flute.

The James Galway of Class Six turned white, then red, then purple. He held up his flute, all twisted and mangled, and called out in a strangulated voice, 'Miss Bingham, Mr Stannard . . . Henry Hooper's sat on my flute. Just *look* at it!' And he started to cry.

All eyes were immediately turned on Henry. It wasn't his fault; he'd been told to sit down so he had. Mr Stannard had so terrified him that he'd not looked behind first. Anyway, Jonathan Pargetter should have been holding on to his instrument. It was stupid leaving flutes on chairs.

Everyone was looking at Henry's bottom. It was large, because Henry was large, and it looked even larger in the skimpy purple shorts. The drums and cymbals in the row behind were having a close look at his rear view, and tittering to each other. Henry felt humiliated.

Mr Stannard sorted it out in five seconds flat, he just ignored Miss Bingham. 'The flute will be repaired and his parents will pay the bill,' he said crisply.

What parents? Henry secretly waved bye-bye to his new bicycle, and tried to picture Cousin Noreen's face when she heard he'd sat on a flute. 'You can listen for today,' the old man informed Jonathan Pargetter. 'You can just follow the music, for this week.'

What music? Henry thought miserably as they all tuned up with awful wailings. He'd left his washboard in the cloakroom anyway, under his anorak, and he certainly wasn't bothering to fetch it now. You could make yourself too cheap with people; Dad always used to tell him that.

Fred Holt had taught him a really good routine on that washboard last night, but he wasn't going to waste it on this lot, even if he was asked.

He wasn't. As soon as Mr Stannard noticed that he was empty-handed he gave him a triangle and sent him to sit with Mavis Bramley.

*

After school the three boys trailed home together through the Springfield Estate, Graham lugging his trombone case, Nev clutching his battered drum, and Henry with the washboard stuck under one arm. Mrs Snell must have been lying in wait behind the standard roses. The minute Graham's hand touched the gate she shot out and grabbed him.

'Thank goodness you're back,' she said sharply, pouncing on him and pulling him inside, like a cat with a mouse. 'I was worried. That Danny Crompton's been hanging round here again today, filthy pig that he is.'

She didn't say a word to Henry and he went off up his own drive. *Filth*, Eunice Snell was obsessed by it. How would she go on if she knew what was hidden in her garage freezer, under the sprouts? Hedgehogs had a lot more fleas than old men.

The sooner he could phone the mad scientist, and take them to the Poly, the better. Anyway, he'd be back in his lab tomorrow, it wasn't long to wait. Meanwhile Henry's mind was occupied with something else. That leg.

He really did wonder whether he ought to get rid of it. He wasn't superstitious but he had an uncanny feeling that it was doing him no good. Everyone was after it, for no apparent reason, and somehow they'd started getting at him too. He was going to let Cousin Noreen have it for her 'sculpt', for free.

But when he got upstairs and looked in his wardrobe the leg had gone. He just couldn't believe it. He threw everything out, clothes, shoes, old wellingtons, burrowing underneath all the mess like an overgrown mole. But there was no doubt about it – his leg had been swiped.

Noreen was out, at the Poly presumably. She'd already started redecorating and the front attic smelt of paint. It was going to be dazzling white. The walls were white, the bookshelves were white, the bedcover was white. It looked like the TV advert for Persil Automatic. In her white granny nightie and her white flour make-up Noreen could have easily disappeared in that room. She'd have just merged into the background.

The sculpt was already under way. There was a big piece of hardboard in the middle of the floor, with mysterious chalk marks on it, and Henry's junk was arranged in little heaps all round the edge, toilet roll tubes and rusty nails, egg boxes and wire coat-hangers. He couldn't see a great work of art coming out of that lot. If he was mad then so was Cousin Noreen.

There was no sign of the leg though, and it wasn't in his room either. He spent ages looking around for it, but it had definitely vanished. After a while he went downstairs and inspected the front door. Now he came to think of it he hadn't used his latch-key at four o'clock. He'd just turned the knob and the door had opened. His mother was supposed to be getting an extra key cut but she'd have forgotten, knowing her. Noreen must have gone off to the Poly and left the door unlocked for young Henry, and in the quiet of the afternoon someone had slipped in, gone up to the attics, and pinched his leg . . .

He climbed up to his room very slowly, keeping his eyes wide open. Two things struck him. One was a smell that hung around the staircase, a dirty human smell that didn't mix with Noreen's new paint and the familiar mustiness of Fir Grove. The other was a series of small dents on the landing lino.

Henry felt like Sherlock Holmes. He got down on his knees and examined the dents minutely. They were little and round and they led across from the bottom of the attic steps to the top of the main staircase. It was rotten lino, brown, cracked, and as old as Henry. But those dents hadn't been there this morning.

Danny Crompton must be a lot more agile than anyone gave him credit for. They'd been made by a wooden leg.

He was going straight round to Egypt Street to recover his property. He wanted his leg back, even if he had decided to donate it to Cousin Noreen. The Blob might be there too; perhaps he and Desperate Dan were working together. But it was nearly five o'clock and his mother would be in at half past, and from the interesting cooking smells drifting up from the kitchen she was obviously in her new 'reformed' mood.

82

There was always a honeymoon period when Mum started a new job. She actually cooked meals and did the washing. He went downstairs thoughtfully. There was a note on the kitchen table saying there was a casserole in the oven and please would he peel some potatoes. They'd be eating at six, when Noreen got home from the Poly.

So there wasn't enough time to get to Egypt Street and back before they both came in, and the casserole smelt rather good. He decided to make the most of it, and stick around. But if there was the least chance of getting out before bedtime he'd got to grab it. Who could tell what that leg might lead to?

14

He slipped out just before eight o'clock. His mother had her feet up in front of the telly and Noreen had shut herself in the front attic. A notice on the door said 'Do Not Disturb'. It didn't look very friendly but she'd explained at tea-time that she was going to work on her sculpt.

'I just want to think about it, Henry,' she'd said owlishly, behind the big moon glasses. 'I need total concentration at this stage. It's nothing personal.'

As he crept downstairs he could hear weird music floating out from under the door, queer spine-chilling music that reminded him of icebergs and great snowy wastes, and polar bears lumbering round in furthest Greenland. It sent shivers down his back. There was Cousin Noreen, all alone in her dazzling white attic, listening, and waiting for inspiration to strike. He somehow couldn't connect music like that with a load of old toilet rolls.

Egypt Street was in the slums, a row of run-down terraced houses, most of them boarded up. It looked just like the pictures of Belfast on the TV news. Danny Crompton lived in the middle at Number Nine.

The front window was at street level. There was nobody around so Henry peeped in. The glass was so filthy he couldn't see anything at all, it was just a browny-orange blur. So he poked his nose through the letterbox.

It was pitch black on the other side, but an awful smell wafted out through the slit, a smell of whisky and greasy hair and sweat. It was the unmistakable Danny Crompton smell, the smell that was still hanging around the stairs at Fir Grove.

And the old man was at home too, unless the radio had been left on to scare burglars away. It was turned up deafeningly loud and the noise was coming from somewhere at the back. Two men were discussing a brand-new opera in which the ladies of the chorus all wore wellington boots. It sounded very intellectual, not Danny Crompton's cup of tea at all.

Henry crept round to the back, through an alley. All the houses had tiny yards but most of the gates had been pinched and the whole place was full of rubble. Egypt Street was obviously waiting for the redevelopment squad with its council bulldozers. But Desperate Dan was an awkward sort of customer, a man who knew his 'rights'. He'd probably stay in Number Nine till they came and flattened it.

Henry made his way through Danny's yard and peeped through the back window. The small room looked like Darnley Tip, piled high with broken furniture and cardboard boxes, with newspapers strewn all over the floor and across various chairs. In the middle of the mess, slumped on a sagging settee, lay Desperate Dan fast asleep. His mouth was open and he was snoring loudly, and on a table in front of him lay Henry's leg.

But it was now in two pieces. The old man had obviously taken a bread knife to it and hacked the foot off. But there was nothing else on the stained table cloth, apart from an empty bottle and two dirty tumblers.

The men on the radio were now having a lively discussion about an 'advanced' modern symphony where the orchestra seemed to consist of three tape recorders and a row of synchronized vacuum cleaners. They played a few bars to the listeners at home, just to give them the flavour. It wouldn't have appealed to Danny Crompton though it might well have interested Cousin Noreen. But the din suited Henry's next move perfectly.

The old man was definitely slipping because he'd gone to sleep without locking his back door. You could just lift the old-fashioned latch and walk in. Anyone could have wandered into Danny's smelly back room and felt up the chimney, or under the floorboards, looking for that fortune he was supposed to have stashed away.

Under cover of the roaring Hoovers Henry opened the door and went inside. The smell was bad enough to turn the strongest stomach, and his heart was pounding away like a road drill. But he was determined to get his leg back.

He took three steps towards the table, grabbed the foot with one hand, the leg with the other, and made off through the back yard, not even stopping to shut the door behind him. He could still hear those men jawing away about the vacuum cleaners as he pelted down Egypt Street towards the main road. But surely no one could have seen him running away from Number Nine with his leg? If there'd been anyone left in that terrace they'd have complained about the noise by now, not to mention the smell.

Noreen's door was wide open when he got back. All his junk was piled up in the middle of the hardboard and she was sitting on the floor, staring at it glassily. The iceberg music had been switched off, and she looked rather dazed.

Henry walked straight in. 'There you are,' he said, dumping

the two pieces in her lap. 'You can have it if you want. I don't suppose it's much use now though, not like that.'

Noreen was dismayed when she saw the leg. 'What on earth did you do that for, Henry?' she said reproachfully. 'You've *ruined* it.'

'I *didn't* do it,' he said fiercely. He'd had enough for one night. 'Someone else did. It was *pinched*. From my room.'

All of a sudden he felt rather shaky, and he flopped down on to Noreen's snow-white mattress. It was only now that he'd realized just what he'd done, and what might have happened. Desperate Dan could have woken up suddenly and gone for him with a broken bottle, or he could have accused him of thieving and stumped off to the nearest police station. Seeing that leg cut into two jagged pieces was starting to give him the creeps, and he didn't like looking at it. It was almost as if Danny Crompton had wanted to do him in. It was like sticking pins into little wax models.

Most people would have laughed at Henry's theories about the leg, but Cousin Noreen didn't. Encouraged by that sympathetic flour-white face behind the glasses he calmed down and told her quite a lot – how Danny had been after his leg from the very beginning, and how he'd tried to take it twice, once in Jubilee Road and once in their very own drive, when Fred had come to the rescue in his Lollocks van.

He didn't tell her about seeing The Blob at Spring Mill though. He wasn't supposed to go near there, and she might tell his mother. But he did show her the dents on the lino, and describe how he'd gone to Egypt Street and found the leg lying on the table.

'You do believe me don't you, Noreen?' he said anxiously, when he'd finished. Now he'd put all the facts together the story sounded absolutely ridiculous. She might think he was making it up.

Cousin Noreen was always very practical. 'Don't tell your mother I left the door open will you?' was her first request. 'I'd got a key but when I went out to the Poly I forgot to put the catch down. We don't want anyone else barging in.'

Henry promised. 'But what about the leg?' he wanted to know. 'That's the important thing. What on earth is he after?'

Noreen looked thoughtful. 'People get passions for things,'

she said dreamily. 'Garden gnomes for instance. Perhaps he just fancied it, Henry, he's obviously a nutcase. There's no accounting for tastes.'

'But why should he cut the foot off? It doesn't make sense to me.'

'Well perhaps he collects feet,' Cousin Noreen said solemnly. She was only trying to help. 'Queen Victoria did; she had the hands and feet of all her children, made in plaster.'

'No,' Henry said solidly. 'That's not it. It can't be.' Noreen was obsessed with Queen Victoria, and she was beginning to irritate him. In spite of the way she'd appeared to listen he suspected she wasn't taking him very seriously. He hardened. He wasn't going to divulge his other theories about the leg, not yet anyway.

'You can have it,' he said abruptly, getting up from the mattress. 'I'm throwing it away otherwise. But I don't suppose you want it now do you?'

Not only did she want it – she offered to pay.

'No, thanks,' Henry said stiffly, going through to his own room. She was just being kind now. He didn't want people's charity.

15

He was clearly offended but Noreen was used to moods. Fred was moody too. And she'd got Clegg blood in her veins too, like Henry. The Cleggs didn't give up easily.

'Here,' she said, following him through the door. 'Here, I'm offering you a pound for it. It's given me an idea and it doesn't matter about the foot. In fact it might help.'

How could it 'help'? Henry eyed her suspiciously. She really was a weirdo. He wasn't sure he liked her any more.

But Noreen had realized that he was upset; it was her fault, something she'd said. He'd obviously set a lot of store by that leg, for some strange reason. She sat on his sag-bag and looked round the cluttered attic, trying to think of something that might cheer him up. He looked so woebegone. She wished she could invent a magic wand out of one of those coat-hangers, one that'd bring his silly father home again. That was the real matter with Henry. But he could be so touchy, like now. It wasn't the right moment to mention his dad.

Her eyes fell upon his notice-board and she got up to look at it. 'I didn't know you wrote poetry, Henry,' she said. 'I love poetry.'

'I don't,' he grunted. 'And it's not poetry. It's just a competition; the Kelly Kitchen people are running it. You've got to write a winning couplet, that's all. But it's more difficult than it sounds.'

Noreen began to read his efforts very carefully. He felt embarassed; it was private really, like her 'sculpt'.

'You've not got very far, have you?' she said, when she'd read everything. She was rather like Nev in some ways – she always said exactly what came into her head, only she usually made a bit more sense.

'No,' Henry answered. 'And I don't think I'm going to bother either. There are too many people going in for it. Mavis Bramley's trying it, in our class. Her dad's an English teacher. I bet he'll do hers.'

'Why do you *want* a dream kitchen?' Noreen wanted to know. 'I like yours as it is; it's, well . . .' She was hunting, unsuccessfully, for the right word.

'A tip,' he said gloomily, before she could finish the sentence.

'No. Well, yes. I suppose it is, a bit. But it's got *character*, Henry. I hate those space-age kitchens, all that glossy formica.'

'I just think Mum could do with something a bit more up to date, that's all,' he said doggedly. 'She gets very restless. Dad was always promising to do it up, but he never got round to it. If it was smartened up she might feel more settled here, don't you see?'

Noreen did, absolutely, and she really wanted to help Henry. He ought to be out enjoying himself with his friends on a nice crisp autumn day like this, not sitting up here planning to win a dream kitchen.

She unpinned the entry form from the notice-board and studied it. 'Look, Henry,' she said at last, 'we can do this between us. There's nothing to say we can't, is there? You write one line and I'll write another. It'll be like playing Consequences. OK?'

'OK,' he said glumly. It sounded a bit odd but he supposed it was better than nothing. He was never going to win that competition on his own, and Cousin Noreen was certainly unusual. There was no telling what a girl like that might come up with; they might beat Mavis Bramley yet.

Just as he was getting his pyjamas on, a piece of paper was pushed under his door. It was a little note from the front attic in artistic black script. Henry read it with interest. 'In the kitchen of life all good dreams start.' That was all.

'The kitchen of *life*?' What was that supposed to mean for heaven's sake? Henry was disappointed. It was worse than his own efforts, and that was saying something.

He thought about it as he did up his buttons and arranged the sheets on his mattress; he was working out rhymes and rhythms in his head, trying to achieve a witty second line. 'In the kitchen of life all good dreams start . . .' he hummed to himself, taking a last look at The Two Ronnies as they settled down for the night. *Kitchen of life.* Honestly, it was pathetic.

Three floors down there was a sudden almighty hammering and banging. Henry pushed his door open a crack, and pricked up his ears. After writing her scintillating first line Noreen had gone downstairs to watch the news with his mother. Now he could hear her pattering along the hall tiles to open the front door. It was probably Fred.

Two minutes later he heard her summoning Mrs Hooper. Two minutes after that his mother was shouting up the stairs. 'Henry? *Henry!* Come down here a minute.'

'I'm asleep,' he called back helplessly. He knew who it was perfectly well. He'd heard a voice coming through the open door, a thin, metallic sort of voice, the kind that carried. It was Eunice Snell.

Mrs Hooper had to shout four times before Henry put in an appearance, and when he finally plucked up the courage to come downstairs it was at a snail's pace, dragging his feet.

It wasn't actually necessary to cross the hall and go to the front door. Mrs Snell was inside and had taken up her position on the bottom step of the staircase. Perhaps she had secret fears that Henry might go off his head, and escape.

But simply looking at her made him much too frightened. She really was mad about what she'd just found in her freezer. Her face was a deep scarlet and her small stringy body was rigid with rage. The hedgehogs had been put into a green Marks and Spencers carrier bag but there were a few spines sticking out, for all his careful wrapping up, and she was swinging it at him, like some kind of primitive battleaxe.

'Are these yours, Henry Hooper?' she said savagely, as he came down the last four steps and drooped before her. 'Yes,' said Henry in a strangled voice, wondering if she was going to have a heart attack; she looked ready to go pop. Then he added, 'I had an arrangement with your Graham.' Well, it was true.

The mere mention of precious Graham seemed to enrage

Eunice even more. Her speech broke down and became a mere babble of words. 'Filth,' and 'Terrible Behaviour' and 'Absolute Disgrace' fell on his ears like a hail of bullets and Henry swayed under the onslaught. Noreen stood on one side of him and his mother stood on the other. He felt like a criminal in the dock.

Listening to Mrs Snell was like watching a river burst through a dam. She said so much, so fast, that mere details were lost on Henry, but he couldn't fail to grasp the essentials. She repeated them so many times.

One: the Snells wouldn't be speaking to the Hoopers any more. (Well, every cloud has a silver lining.)

Two: their Graham wouldn't be coming to school with

Henry any more. (Who cared? He was a pain in the neck anyway.)

Three: if anything like this happened again she might have to report it to the police station in Jubilee Road. Henry did realize, didn't he, that what he'd done had constituted a real health hazard? Hedgehogs were riddled with fleas, and she did have a baby in the house. Anything could have happened if this business had continued very much longer.

Threat Number Three sobered Henry up slightly, though his mother and Noreen, flanking him on each side like two prison warders, hadn't said a word since Eunice had opened her mouth. They'd seemed robbed of speech by the force of the blast. Frankie was a nice little thing actually, when there were no screams coming from that amazing letter box mouth.

But as for telling the *police* . . . What were they supposed to do about a handful of hedgehogs in Eunice Snell's freezer? They did have some weird complaints coming in. Henry felt quite sorry for them sometimes.

After saying quite a lot more about being bad neighbours, and letting the place go to rack and ruin, the Towering Inferno stormed off down the drive. The carrier bag had been hung on the knob at the bottom of the staircase and Henry just stood there dumbly, with 'Filth', 'Disgrace' and 'Terrible' ringing in his ears.

Noreen and his mother were still at their posts, flanking him on each side, unable to believe it either. It was a calm evening and sounds carried. Nobody moved until they heard the click of Snells' front gate. Then, 'Henry,' Noreen whispered, 'what on earth were you doing storing dead hedgehogs in that poor woman's freezer?' And his mother was saying, in a flat, weary kind of voice, 'Henry, I give up on you, love, I really do.'

He tried to explain about the ad in the *Star*, how he'd tried to contact the mad scientist at the Poly because he needed the cash, and how four hedgehogs might bring in two or three pounds, how he'd wrapped them hygienically in cling-film, and stored them in polythene bags as instructed.

But Noreen and his mother didn't appear to be listening. What was more, they seemed to have the greatest difficulty standing upright; in fact, they were clinging on to each other for support, and Noreen was laughing so much that the tears ran down her face. 'Hedgehog stew,' she kept giggling. 'That woman nearly had hedgehog *stew*.'

Henry had never seen anyone laugh till they cried before, and his mother was most peculiar too. He couldn't get any sense out of her at all. She just banged round the kitchen, repeating Mrs Snell's various threats, Not Speaking, Telling The Police, Their Graham Going To School With His Dad From Now On, and all the time her shoulders were shaking with laughter.

Henry's punishment was a cold beef sandwich and two slices of cake. When he'd eaten them he decided to go to bed of his own free will, feeling totally bewildered. Noreen and his mother were still chattering and laughing down in the kitchen.

He climbed the stairs very slowly though, partly because he was tired and partly because they'd started discussing the Snells more seriously. His mother wasn't really amused any more; perhaps all that silly tittering had been for his benefit. Eunice had been in such an awful state, waving those hedgehogs, any child would have been unnerved by it.

'She's a bit obsessional,' he heard her telling Noreen. 'The house is like a museum, in spite of the baby. I've never seen anything like it, you could eat your dinner off the floor in that kitchen. Mind you, if George Snell wasn't so keen to "get on" in the firm, and make his million by forty, I mean, if he was *around* more, she wouldn't have so much time to kill. Even with the baby she's always cleaning and tidying up, and Graham's going the same way, I think.'

'Yes,' Noreen said thoughtfully. 'Henry said he wouldn't play with his new football in case it got dirty; I could hardly believe it.'

'Oh, I can,' Mrs Hooper said drily. 'I feel sorry for Graham. He's such a nervous little thing. She makes him like that.'

Henry quickened his pace up to the attics and got into bed quickly. If Mrs Snell was so obsessed with dirt and germs he'd done rather an awful thing, storing those hedgehogs in her freezer, double-wrapped in polythene or not. Hygiene was obviously very important to her for some reason, and it must have been like someone breaking into a mansion and committing a burglary on a grand scale.

What was the survival level of a hedgehog flea, he wondered, snuggling down. Flies got into their old fridge sometimes, through the broken door, and they survived for ages if you didn't get them out. You'd find them days later sometimes, wandering drunkenly about as the cold slowed them down. So if flies could survive in a twenty-year-old fridge what might have happened to a hundred full-blown hedgehog fleas in a very modern freezer?

He hoped Mrs Snell wasn't busy throwing everything away. She'd been so enraged he could just see it, and if she did they'd get the bill. She wouldn't wait till morning either, she'd be at it *now*. It'd be a month's shopping at Tesco's at the very least and where would the money come from for that?

He just hadn't thought enough about that arrangement with Graham Snell. If Dad were here he'd never have embarked on such a crazy venture; there were surely less complicated ways of making a few pounds.

Poor Mrs Snell though. As he warmed up, and began to feel drowsy, that thin, bewildered voice rang round and round in his head. When he drifted off to sleep at last Henry's cheeks were quite pink with shame.

Noreen offered to take the bag of hedgehogs to the Poly herself, when she went to classes, but Henry had quite lost heart by next morning. He left them outside, by the dustbins, and when she came back in the late afternoon they buried them all under the old lilac tree.

Noreen said it was a pity to waste them and that they'd eventually rot down and manure the soil, and that'd be good for the tree. Lilacs, she explained, were very greedy feeders.

16

Two days later he saw lights again in Spring Mill. This time the rain woke him, hammering on the roof, and he got up to look through his window. He liked stormy weather.

Henry was cautious by nature. It was a filthy night and the view over Darnley was blurred; the wobbling motorway lights were turning into orange streaks and running down the glass. But he stayed there for a good ten minutes, watching and waiting, and making sure.

There was most definitely somebody snooping around. They'd got a flash-light and it was bluey-grey, wavering in and out of the crumbling walls then going off altogether. Perhaps The Blob was back, doing his Securicor act.

He fell asleep plotting to skip school next morning. His throat was a bit sore anyway, and with luck it might turn into a cold. Even if it didn't he was still going to miss a few lessons. He just couldn't face Graham Snell for one thing, not after that upset with his mother, and there was too much to do round here anyway. He wasn't going to be rushed.

Nev Hodgkinson often played truant and he usually wrote his own absence notes, though Miss Bingham didn't seem too bothered about getting letters from home; she was more interested in 'creative self expression'. 'Just as long as you're better, dear,' she'd beamed at him when he'd handed in his forged note last Tuesday morning. Everyone knew that Nev was the biggest skiver in the class. It'd all change after Christmas, when The Beast came back.

Anyhow, Henry was definitely truanting tomorrow morning. It was daring for him though – he was usually quite law-abiding. He drifted off thinking about the Return of the Blob. All this criminal activity was definitely catching.

Early next day he slipped a note through Nev's letter box explaining about his cold. Then he went back home and crept upstairs again. It was only seven-fifteen but his mother was already in the bath, singing lustily. She'd be out of the house by eight and his toast would be left to get cold on the kitchen table. As soon as the new job lost its glamour she'd go back to sleeping late, and dragging herself out of bed at the very last minute. But while the honeymoon period lasted she'd get herself to work early.

It was just as well for Henry, otherwise she might wait around to see him off to school. And it was a good thing that Cousin Noreen wasn't a morning person either, otherwise she'd be up too, and asking awkward questions.

He'd decided to try to get into the foundations of Spring Mill, and he wanted to do it in the daylight. The Blob – if that's who it was – definitely kept going back there, and the only foolproof way of getting inside the buildings was up through the cellars, unless you were an expert at picking locks, and Henry wasn't.

But he was dismayed when he inspected their secret hole in the wall, down by the canal bank. It was thickly overgrown with last year's brambles and he'd need something like Eunice Snell's giant secateurs to cut through them all. He pulled a couple away and saw the soft inside blackness of the mill behind. So they'd not concreted it over then. Well, that was something. But even if he came back with clippers, or a big knife, he doubted that he'd be able to squeeze through that hole again. He'd grown a lot since last summer.

He rearranged the brambles, got back on his bike, and pedalled round to the mill yard. Then he dumped the fairy-cycle in some long grass behind a wall and crept across to the huge iron gates.

Just inside, where the old motor bike had been, there were fresh oil patches, purpley-blue splodges that gleamed wetly in the watery sunlight. So The Blob had been back then, even if he wasn't here now. He'd put one foot inside the entrance when the buzz of an engine stopped him in his tracks. He scuttled back to the crumbling wall and crouched down, then he stuck his nose out to see what was going on.

A smart green van with 'Pollitt's Estates' painted on the side in white pulled up and stopped outside the mill entrance. Three men got out, two oldish ones and a youth, and began unloading tools and drills, and a huge coil of shiny new barbed wire was dumped in the wet grass.

It had all the air of an official operation. Pollitt's men were dressed identically, in smart green boiler suits, and they'd obviously been sent here to make Spring Mill secure yet again. The young one immediately shinned up to the top of the left-hand wall and inspected it. 'Chuck us a hammer, Cyril,' he shouted down bossily, 'the brickwork's not too bad. I'll make a start here I think.'

On the ground more hammers were clanging and great locks being screwed into position. It was hard to understand *why* though – anything worth nicking must have gone years ago. Old Man Pollitt was just another Eunice Snell, over-cautious, and neurotic about break-ins. Her first job, when they'd moved in next door, had been to get a great yellow burglar alarm fitted over the front porch. There it was, lurking behind the wisteria like an angry wasp, though there was nothing you'd want to steal from Snells', not even their Graham's chintzy chair. But Mrs Snell got so nervous about everything.

The three Pollitt henchmen whistled as they worked, and the young one on top of the wall had a radio tuned in to some pop programme. Vaguely encouraged, Henry crept out of hiding and walked up to the gates, whistling too. Perhaps he could ask this boy a few leading questions, he could even tell the older ones about the lights he'd seen, during the night.

But the minute they saw him all three men stopped what they were doing and stared. The one on the wall snapped his radio off and shouted down quite savagely, 'Hey! Sod off will you! What the hell do you think you're doing, hanging round here?'

Henry didn't like that. Neither would Old Man Pollitt. He was a pillar of Green Street Methodist Chapel, where Gran went, and he wouldn't approve of that kind of language, not from someone he was paying good money to. He'd have to watch it, that boy would.

'I said *Sod Off!*' the youth repeated; he seemed much more against Henry than the other two and he was getting ready to climb down off the wall, to show that he really meant business, when Cyril interrupted from down below.

'Come on, mate,' he said. 'The lad's not doing any harm. He's only watching. No law against that, you know.'

But Cyril knew perfectly well that, in spite of the smart van and the boiler suits, they shouldn't really have been there at all, securing the mill like this. The case was coming on in court again next week. Old Pollitt had clever solicitors but they might not get away with it. If they lost he'd be out of a job, along with his old pal Frank here. The apprentice was some distant relation of Pollitt's wife; that'd be why he was throwing his weight around. He didn't want this boy hanging about watching, then running off to tell someone what he'd seen. He was right in a way, it wouldn't sound too good in court. They ought to get rid of him.

No need. The apprentice was on the ground now, his face only inches away from Henry's nose. 'OK. Now just clear off, will you,' he muttered, through clenched teeth. 'Just Get Lost. *Quick.*' He was a Pollitt after all, sort of. They didn't want this episode in the papers, and he whispered as much to the two older men.

The three of them closed in on Henry, the youth with his hammer, Cyril with a great spanner, Frank with his hands full of nails.

'Why aren't you at school?' Cyril said. 'You should be. And you're on private land, son. Did you know that? You're trespassing and you're playing hookey as well. I'd buzz off if I were you.'

'*Fast,*' added the youth aggressively, waving his hammer.

Henry was frightened for a moment – they were just a bit too near him with those heavy tools. He saw a real row developing, and his face getting smashed to a pulp. Awful things happened in Darnley sometimes.

'Sod off,' the boy with the hammer said, for the third time, and at last Henry retreated, and slunk away, back to his fairy-

cycle. He could hear the two older ones arguing about 'getting a move on in case anybody turned up' but the apprentice was already back on the wall, a satisfied smile on his flattish, empty face. He was knocking those nails in as if he was driving them into Henry's skull.

It took quite a while for him to get back on his bike again. He was shaking with nerves and, anyway, he was still curious, and distance gave him a certain safety. The pop music had been turned up quite loud now, and they were all hammering and banging away.

He watched for a few more minutes then pedalled off, feeling frustrated, stupid and small. Legally or illegally the enormous rusty gates had been padlocked yet again, and now the walls were festooned with wreaths of barbed wire. Neither he nor The Blob would ever get into Spring Mill now, not unless they went on a starvation diet and stuffed themselves down that hole.

He'd more or less decided to go into school and tell Miss Bingham that his bad sore throat had miraculously cleared up when another idea took his fancy. Why didn't he walk down to the Market and have a chat with old Bulldog at the pet shop? He'd be quiet this morning, and Henry wanted a few ideas. Rabbits were *out* because Nev was so keen to palm a couple off on him, which definitely meant trouble. But the gerbils were getting a bit smelly up in his attic, especially when all the windows had to be kept shut during cold spells.

Noreen had suggested a few fish; soothing, she'd said, and beautiful. Would Bulldog swap The Two Ronnies for a little tank and a couple of angel fish? She'd promised to go halves with him if he got anywhere in his negotiations.

He walked rapidly towards the town centre in his shabby patched jeans, his scruffy Canals sweatshirt and his down-at-heel shoes, not really thinking about school, or whether someone Important might see him. Henry was single-minded and he wanted *action*, something to put the sting of those foul Pollitt people out of his head. Fish could do that, two lovely rainbow-coloured fish gliding about in a dimly lit tank . . .

But as luck would have it his route took him very near the town flats where Dad and Sheila lived, twelve floors up in a mini skyscraper, a bit like a fish tank itself, in a way, an up-ended box painted yellow. There were three blocks, all the same bright lemon colour, towering up over the old parish church like something made from giant Lego. A flat up there wouldn't suit Henry at all. He didn't like heights.

Dad might be there *now*. How could he walk straight past and visit old Bulldog to cadge a couple of fish, and not go and see his own father? He was almost at the entrance to the Covered Market when he suddenly twisted away, recrossed the new town centre gardens, and walked round to the back of Dad's block. He went past the dustbins and began toiling up the stairs. He wasn't using that express lift in the front hall; it had stuck once, the day he'd come to tea with Sheila, and he didn't trust it any more.

Their back door was painted a trendy sludge green and it had a large keyhole as well as a Yale lock. It cost money to rent a town centre flat and everyone was neurotic about burglars. There was nobody about, so Henry crouched down and peeped through. Looking through keyholes was becoming a habit.

He couldn't see much at first but when his eyes had stopped watering he made out the shape of a pine table covered with washing, and a chair with a red and white shirt draped over the back. Mum had given Dad that shirt.

He couldn't see anything else though, however hard he screwed his eyes up; just the washing, and some dirty cups and saucers, and a crumpled newspaper. Sheila Howarth wouldn't have allowed that – she was a demon scrubber and tidier like Mrs Snell. It really was true then. She'd walked out.

Henry knocked for ages but nobody came except a moth-eaten ginger cat that bounded down from the thirteenth floor and rubbed itself ecstatically against his legs. That wouldn't be Sheila's, she didn't like animals. He really couldn't understand why his father had ever moved in with her.

He was half-way down the back stairs again when he collided with someone coming up. At first all he saw was a pair of feet. Could they be Dad's? Henry took size nine shoes already and his father's were like herring-boxes. But these feet were small and narrow, and so was the face of the owner, crumpled and little and about sixty years old. The man carried a mop and a bucket of soapy disinfectant and he was looking at Henry as if he'd crawled out from under a stone.

'What do *you* want?' he said. The voice that came out of the wizened little mouth was loud and quite threatening. Then he saw Henry's size nine shoes, all caked with mud from the canal bank, and the size nine footprints all over his clean stairs. Henry wasn't too fussy about wiping his feet and the old caretaker had just been all the way to the bottom for some clean rinsing water.

'I was looking for my father,' Henry said loudly, before anything was said about the muddy footprints. 'I don't suppose you've seen him have you?'

The old man took a crumpled list from his overall pocket, and looked down it. 'What's the name?' he grunted. He wanted this boy off his clean premises. It could have been worse – he *could* have come in through the front door and upset the residents. He looked a bit scruffy, and why wasn't he at school?

'Hooper.'

'Hooper ... P. R.? Shares with an S. Howarth? Number 12C?'

'That's it.'

As he stood there something funny was happening to Henry's throat. It was like that time the fish bone had stuck sideways at Grandma Clegg's and he'd nearly choked. Mum had half killed him, thumping him on the back to try and dislodge it. Hearing the old man mention Sheila Howarth and his dad in one breath like that, with no feeling whatever in the little screwed-up blue eyes, and no sympathy, was just the same. Though why *should* he be sorry? 'It goes on all the time in these town flats.' Mum had explained that herself at the time.

'He's my *dad*!' he wanted to scream down the long echoing stair-well. 'He's my *dad* and he's left my mum for this awful woman that cleans up after him all the time. He's my *dad*, and I want him back.'

The old man was pushing past to get at Henry's big muddy marks with his mop and bucket.

'Look,' said Henry standing plumb in the middle of a step. If he refused to budge he'd just have to be given a hearing. 'Have you any idea where he's gone? Or where *she's* gone? I knocked and knocked but nobody answered.'

'Wouldn't expect them to, would you, not at this time in the morning? Won't they be at work? Look, Sonny Jim – and move your feet will you – it says here that the rent's still being paid. That's all I can tell you.'

'But it's all ... it's all such a mess in there,' Henry burst out suddenly. 'I mean there's –'

'Ah *ha*, been spying on them have you? Got your own key have you? Now that really *is* against the rules.' The caretaker had produced a little black notebook from a rear pocket and was licking a stub of pencil. He was doing his policeman act now.

'You'd better give me your name, mate, and your address. Can't have this sort of palaver going on, not here. The residents don't like this sort of thing at all. Name?'

'It's Hen – No!' said Henry suddenly. 'I've *not* been spying. I just looked through the keyhole and noticed what a mess it all was. No law against that is there?' Hadn't this peculiar old man got the message yet? *He wanted his dad,* that was all, yet here he was, being treated like some kind of criminal.

The notebook and pencil were suddenly put away and the caretaker grabbed his bucket and mop. 'All right, all right, but there's nobody at home is there?' and he pushed past Henry on his way to floor fifteen. 'Now just *shove off* will you, son,' he said brusquely, over his shoulder. 'These are prestige properties. You're going to get me into trouble with the boss, hanging round here.' There'd have certainly been trouble if Mr Goldman, who owned the flats, had seen this boy in the front entrance hall, sitting among all the potted plants and glossy magazines. He needed smartening up a bit; his mother ought to look after him better, even if the dad had scarpered with this Sheila woman.

Spying through keyholes. This modern education lark was a washout. A boy like that'd have been given the strap in his day.

It took Henry quite a long time to negotiate all those steps. They were slippy from the soapy water and his eyes were full of tears. He'd wanted his dad, that was all. He'd been within inches of his door and he'd wanted him. And that horrible caretaker had treated him like something the cat'd brought in; he'd been almost as nasty as the Pollitt brigade. He wouldn't go back to those flats in a hurry; he'd ask Mum where his dad was.

He'd gone right off visiting old Bulldog now. Noreen could wait for her soothing fish tank, he'd only get into an argument about cages and gerbils and 'gluts'. Instead he decided to go and visit Mr Schofield off Jubilee Road. He was the one old man who was always glad to see Henry, and guess what – he'd just found that gold watch, still in his jeans pocket. Good thing Mum hadn't washed them yet this week.

He ought to go back to school, but he couldn't really wander along in the middle of lessons. He'd got to go back and put his purple horrors on first, and he'd be much less conspicuous turning up at dinner time when they were all in the playground, note or no note. He might as well go to Schofield's and see if the old man would give him anything for his watch.

But the shop was still boarded up, and so was the door, and now there was an official-looking notice hammered to the boards. 'All inquiries to Darnley 50370'. It was perfectly obvious that Mr Schofield had gone for good.

Why though? Henry thought about it as he wandered back through the cobbled alley. It surely couldn't be that break-in? He'd had dozens of them since opening his own shop thirty years ago. Jewellers always did, it was a risky business.

He was going to miss old Mr Schofield and he was disappointed on his own account too. Nobody else was going to relieve him of that watch. There was another money-making scheme gone to pot.

Henry took a long time getting to sleep that night. Everything had gone wrong since the minute he'd got out of bed. Pollitt's lot had been foul to him, especially that young apprentice, and they'd made Spring Mill harder to penetrate than Fort Knox, with all their nuts and bolts. The caretaker at the flats had been equally foul; worse, in a way, screwing up his tiny piggy eyes and pushing at Henry's feet with a mop, as if he'd been some kind of smelly rubbish that'd got to be disposed of quick.

Where was his friend, Mr Schofield? He'd have been kind. And where were his dad and Sheila Howarth? And why didn't anyone *tell* him anything? It was *his* dad, and he wanted him. Not for anything in particular; he just wanted to see him.

He squirmed about, trying to get comfortable on his mattress, but he knew quite well that sleep would be a long time coming because the events of the last few hours were going round and round in his head like a whirligig at a fair.

All in all it had been one of the most miserable days of Henry's whole life.

17

'Poor Mr Schofield's died,' his mother announced as they sat round the kitchen table on the Friday night, eating Noreen's sloppy mutton curry.

'Dead?' said Henry, turning as white as chalk, the forkful of curry half-way to his mouth suddenly freezing in mid-air.

'Dead and buried I'm afraid, chick. They give me the obituary notice to type out in the office. Not very tactful of them was it, but they weren't to know he was a good friend of your grandad's, I don't suppose.'

Henry's white face was rapidly turning greenish. With his mouth opening and shutting like that, and his cheeks still stuffed with food, he was rapidly beginning to resemble a frog. 'Dead?' he repeated, and the rice he'd just swallowed seemed to have stuck half-way down his throat like a great gobstopper. 'But he *can't* be dead, Mum; I mean, well, I *saw* him last week. I was talking to him.'

Mrs Hooper shot to her feet in alarm when she saw him change colour so rapidly and she was now trying to get a drink of water down him, with Noreen making cajoling noises at her elbow. She wasn't at all certain what she ought to say next. Big Henry was quite a sensitive plant in his way; he was a worrier, for all his size nine shoes and his big freckled face. And he'd been fond of Mr Schofield.

'Well it was a heart attack I think, love. You know, here one minute, gone the next. It's a good way to go, Henry, when you're old. Better than suffering on like your Grandad Clegg.'

Henry supposed it was. 'Suffering on' sounded awful. Fred Holt was trying to persuade Noreen to start going on marches now, and he'd not only painted a big black badge on her dazzling white wall, but he'd given her a 'comic' book about how they'd all be 'suffering on' if The Bomb dropped. It had quite terrified Henry.

He went off upstairs without finishing his curry, and when Noreen appeared a few minutes later she found him stretched out on his mattress staring up at the ceiling. She came straight in and settled down on his sag-bag for a chat.

'How could he *die*, just like that?' he blurted out suddenly. Somehow he couldn't say it to his mother, but he could to Noreen.

'Well, perhaps his heart was broken,' she said mysteriously. 'It can happen, you know. People have shocks, and they just give up the will to live, when they're old. Doctors'll tell you that.'

'What do you mean?' said Henry. It didn't sound a bit like Arthur Schofield, he'd been such a cheery old bloke.

'Well between you and me, Henry, there's more to it than meets the eye. I think so anyway. Your mum knows quite a bit about it; I heard her telling Gran on the phone. The whole story was supposed to be going in to the *Examiner*, and your mum saw it or something, in the office. It wasn't printed in the end because he'd just dropped dead the day before, in Rochdale Road. So they only printed the obituary.'

'But *what story*?' Henry said irritably. He'd got over his initial shock now, and she seemed to be talking in riddles.

'Well I don't know the details,' she explained, more cautious than ever. 'But he'd been given some stuff for valuation, I think, and when he had that break-in it disappeared along with everything else. I don't know what it was but it must have been worth a bomb, and it should have been in the safe. That's the thing, it *wasn't*, and the insurance won't pay up, so it's all a bit of a scandal because the owner wanted *him* to pay up of course. Old Mrs Schofield's terribly upset about it, naturally; she's been telling Gran. She's sure that's what brought on the heart attack.'

Henry didn't say anything else but all this made sense. He remembered the old man crying as he bent down to pick up his eyeglass, and how that had told him there was something else wrong, something big. He'd been right for once.

When Noreen had gone back next door to start work on her 'sculpt' he stayed on his mattress wondering whether that reward was still on offer. It was callous of him, in the circumstances, but he just couldn't help thinking about it, and how his leg might be involved, and The Blob. If he could find out what had happened to that missing jewellery, or whatever it was, he'd not only be doing something for old Arthur Schofield – he'd be in the money at last.

He must get his mother on her own, to find out more about what had actually happened. Then he could do his own bit of private detective work. He couldn't raise money for Darnley Miners' on his clapped-out fairy-cycle, and he couldn't bring Arthur Schofield back from the dead, or his grandad. But he could do this, and it'd be like helping them both.

18

But Henry got nowhere fast.

'Mum, what *is* happening about Schofield's shop?' he said the next afternoon. He came straight out with it when she was in the kitchen, trying to roll some pastry out for a meat pie. 'Here, can I do that? You've put too much fat in, that's why it's all crumbly.'

Mrs Hooper stood back quite willingly and let Henry line the pie-dish. Baking wasn't her ideal way of spending her precious half day off from the *Examiner* but she was feeling guilty about Henry. His dad was a good cook and he'd taught him a few tricks, but they'd lived on junk food since the break-up, till Cousin Noreen had arrived with her 'experiments'. But she was eating out with Fred tonight.

His mother watched him patiently roll the sticky grey lump out again, and hoped he'd stop asking awkward questions about Schofield's. But he didn't; he just went on and on at her like a dentist's drill.

'Chick, I don't *know*,' she said helplessly, as he took her through the third degree, filling the grey pastry shell with even greyer mince and onions. 'I can only tell you – and this is strictly between ourselves – that there's going to be a prosecution, and until it's all out in the open the *Examiner* staff are all sworn to secrecy. That obviously includes me, so your mum's got to keep mum, chick. Get it?'

She smiled at him rather nervously; there was no way of getting a grin out of Henry today, only one of his dark suspicious looks. He couldn't really understand it, even now.

'But you can tell *me*, Mum, surely? It's only *me*. Who am I going to tell, for Heaven's sake?'

'Nobody, love, nobody in this world. But suppose the police came round and asked me point blank if I'd said anything. I'd . . . well, I'd have to tell them, wouldn't I?'

Henry gave her one of his shrewd sideways glances. He didn't quite like all this cageyness on his mother's part. He didn't *mistrust* her exactly, there was just something he couldn't get to the bottom of. It couldn't be anything to do with him after all. She didn't know about Danny Crompton's obsession with that leg, or The Blob and the face at the window, and she certainly didn't know about his visits to Spring Mill. Even if she did, she wouldn't have connected them with the raid on Schofield's shop. How could she?

When Noreen dashed in at six to get changed for her night out with Fred, Henry managed to snatch five minutes' conversation with her up in the attic. He held a rapid interrogation as she stood in front of the mirror, patching up her floury white make-up and renewing the boot-black mascara.

He was feeling quite hurt by his mother's silence and he didn't believe that bit about the police coming round either. His own mother, and she couldn't even trust him.

'Look, Hen, if they've all been told to keep their mouths shut that's it, isn't it? It can't exclude your mother.'

'But it's only *me*,' Henry repeated helplessly. 'Surely she can trust *me*?' After yesterday, the day of the Great Brush Off, he just felt like crying. And he was only trying to get at the truth. Would nobody tell him anything?

'Honestly, Hen – fasten this chain for me will you – honestly, Hen, I should think, knowing your mum, she's forgotten all the details already, if she ever knew them. She's got a mind like a sieve, you know that; I'm *sure* it's nothing personal.'

'All right, all right, but don't call me Hen,' he said peevishly. It was bad enough when his mother called him 'chick'.

When Noreen had roared off with Fred in his Lollocks van and Mum had switched *Emmerdale Farm* off Henry decided that the Time Had Come. Not to continue the interrogation about the Schofield mix-up – he'd given up on that for now – but to find out where his dad was. It was a thousand times more important anyway.

110

But the minute he mentioned the name Mrs Hooper's eyes filled up with tears. It always happened but Henry felt he couldn't be fobbed off any longer. He had his feelings too, so he just crashed on callously.

'Where *is* he, Mum?' he kept repeating. Three times he said it and three times his mother gave him the same reply, muffled, through a grubby old handkerchief. 'Dunno, chick, you know him, you know how he wanders. I suppose he could be anywhere.'

'Mum, I want to *see* him, and I want to know where he *is*.' This fourth time Henry was almost shouting. That did it. There'd been enough rows in that house to last a lifetime, and now mother and son were at it.

'I don't know, Henry, and that's the truth,' and Mrs Hooper burst into tears and wept into the handkerchief.

This time the tears didn't upset Henry all that much. He was too flabbergasted. 'But *how* can't you know?' he said. It was his dad and he wanted the facts. How on earth could she be so vague about someone he loved, someone *she* loved, in spite of Sheila Howarth. It was as if she'd somehow lost him, like last week's washing.

Mrs Hooper sniffed, stopped crying, and gave the fire a poke. 'All right, chick, I'll tell you what I know. It's not much and it doesn't lead anywhere, so don't get excited. I . . . I should have told you before but, oh, what was the *use*? We're stuck, chick, stuck here, unless that pig-headed father of yours pulls himself together a bit.'

Henry didn't much like hearing his father called pig-headed. His mother could be pretty stupid at times too, but at least she was going to spill the beans, so he'd better not say anything, in case she suddenly changed her mind.

'Well, Sheila Howarth's walked out on him, that's the first thing.' Mrs Hooper sniffed; she was still crying quietly into the handkerchief but for some reason she thought that Henry couldn't see what was going on. It was a big blue handkerchief, one of Dad's.

'Well, that's good isn't it?' said Henry, hutching up to her on the battered settee. It meant he was on his own anyway; all right, twelve floors up in Legoland, but still, it had got to be better than having someone like Sheila Howarth trying to

force a wedding ring on his finger, if that's what was really happening, and it *was*, according to the Grandma–Noreen grapevine.

'I don't know,' said Mum. 'Is it? He's not at the flats; I went round again last week and the caretaker hadn't seen him for days. Someone had been paying the rent and that's all he knew.'

Henry nearly told her about his own visit to the flats but he decided against it in the end. She'd calmed down now so she just might tell him a little more, but not if he let on how foul that old caretaker had been to him, telling him to shove off and everything, and going on about his filthy shoes. Mrs Hooper was fierce about Henry; she was like a tiger with an ailing cub when someone really got it in for him, at school. She'd be off to Legoland like a shot, to see that caretaker, if Henry said anything.

Then there was the small matter of his having played truant all morning . . .

Henry sat up close on the settee and waited.

'Where *is* he, Mum, if he's not in the flats?'

'I don't know. I phoned him at the Council offices but they said he'd taken sick leave and wasn't coming back for a month.'

'*Sick* leave?'

'That's what they said.'

'But, but is he all right, Mum?' A pang had suddenly shot right through Henry and he was beginning to feel sick with nerves. Everyone seemed to be dying off round here. 'What if he's really *ill*?'

'It's nothing Henry, nothing. We'd have heard if it was, believe you me,' and she put her arm round him firmly and kicked at the miserable fire. Dad was always telling her off about that, about how it cracked the shoe leather and led to big repairs. She needed him, oh, for so many things.

'I'm sure he's all right, chick,' she went on. 'But he's been under the weather since he's been on his own.'

'What d'you mean, *under the weather*?'

'Well, a bit depressed. The doctor put him on a tonic and things, and told him to have a few weeks off work.'

'So where's he been then?' Henry couldn't think of anything more depressing than being on your own twelve floors up in the Legoland flats, with visits from Sheila Howarth, specially to spy on you.

'I'm not sure, but he did go to your Uncle Bill's, I do know that. Gran told me. He might be still there for all I know.'

News of Uncle Bill made Henry feel rather better. He was Dad's kid brother and he lived outside Hull on a caravan site. He was a kind of dropout. Henry had enjoyed his odd visits to Uncle Bill; he liked long rainy walks, and cooking things over fires, and he wasn't fussy about the use of soap and water. His caravan was stuffed with books and he was supposed to be writing one. It never seemed to get finished though.

'Why don't we go and see if he's there?' Henry said, after a silence. A great longing to see his father's face had swept over him, filling him with a sudden, intense pain. He just wanted to talk to him about things, he wanted to hear his voice. 'We could go on the bus this weekend,' he went on. 'If

113

he's not there it doesn't matter, does it? We can use our family bus ticket. Go on, Mum. *Please*.'

She was clearly taken aback at this suggestion. '*No*, Henry,' she said, very firmly at first, then 'Well, let's leave it, love, for a few days anyway. I mean, he *might* turn up here. Miracles do happen.' She wanted him back as well, Henry knew that.

Miracles. Not nowadays. The only shred of hope was a bundle of letters shoved behind the copper kettle, in Dad's handwriting, to his mum. One had lost its envelope and it began 'My dear Ivy . . .' So it couldn't be about solicitors, not that one anyway. Perhaps Cousin Noreen was right and he *was* jumping the gun a bit, thinking Dad might never come back. Perhaps there *was* 'always hope'.

He didn't ask any more questions but he kept himself awake till Noreen came home and reported the whole conversation to her at midnight. She just told him to stop probing and to leave his mother alone. It didn't take much to upset Mrs Hooper – she'd been discussing that with Fred, in the van.

'Grown-ups have feelings as well as children, Henry,' she said quite sharply. 'You think it's the other way round, but it's not, you know. Your mum's had quite a few letters from your father, and some of them have upset her. It's still hopeful though, in a funny way.'

'I know about the letters,' said Henry. 'They're behind the copper kettle. But why say it's *hopeful* when they do that to her?' Henry understood less and less now.

'Look, Hen, it's nearly one in the morning. Stop rabbiting on, will you, and go to bed. I'm an optimist and I keep my ears very close to the ground, and I believe it's going to be *all right*. See?'

'It's all right for *you*,' Henry said bleakly, 'they aren't your parents, and just stop calling me Hen will you. It's getting on my nerves.' He'd had a really bad evening.

'Sorry,' Noreen said humbly. 'Sorry, old fruit.' She didn't seem at all offended. She just blinked at him behind the big moon glasses and told him yet again to 'wait and see'.

19

For a long time waiting was all he could do, about everything. Cousin Noreen was installed in the front attic and busy with her classes at the Poly, life settled down into its old routine again, and everything became ordinary and flat.

It was quieter too because The Snells weren't speaking to them, on account of the hedgehogs. Every morning Graham left for school in his dad's new Ford Granada, sweeping past Henry and the Hodgkinsons as they plodded along to the bus stop. Well, that was all right. He could have more fun with Nev and The Ugly Sisters without Graham Snell there, spreading disapproval, and since the gerbil episode Nev had been rather anxious to please. His mum must have told him off for being such a cheat.

He was still pressing Henry to accept two rabbits but Henry wouldn't have them, so one day a pound was produced, for the non-appearance of Eunice Snell's babies. Henry put it in his pocket before he changed his mind. It would be Mrs Hodgkinson's pound, *guilt money*. But he was still having it.

Added to the cash Noreen had given him for the leg and all the other rubbish he now had £3.44. He'd been hoping his pocket money might start flowing again, now his mother had a job with the *Examiner*, but all he ever heard about was 'final demands' as she paid off the gas and the electricity. There was no way of getting a new bike out of her this side of Christmas, and a second-hand one would cost a lot more than £3.44.

The sponsored cycle ride for Darnley Miners came and went. It was depressing. Henry stood at the end of Willow Way one Saturday afternoon and watched them all pedal by, *en route* to the moors on their new Raleigh Winners and their flashy Japanese racers. He felt so miserable he went round to Nev's and they watched a video of *The Killer Bees* to cheer themselves up. Nev hadn't been on the ride either – he'd ruined his back tyre doing skids along Springfield Avenue and his dad had thrown a fit, and said he wasn't paying for it, not even for a charity race.

As he watched the bees slowly killing off everyone in the United States rebellion stirred in Henry's heart and he suddenly leaned forward and pushed in the 'pause' button. It wasn't Real Life at all, and they'd seen it about fifty times already. Even the best videos got boring after a while.

'*Hey*,' said Nev grumpily, 'this is the best bit. What are you doing stopping it now, you great nit.'

'Well, I've got to go home soon,' said Henry, glancing up at the mantelpiece clock. 'And there's something I want to ask you. It's important.'

'Go on then,' Nev said impatiently, his eyes still glued to the screen. 'Get on with it.' Now it was frozen the scene where the girl's face got slowly eaten away by the bees was becoming more and more interesting. You could do some good things with videos.

'Well I want to go back to Spring Mill,' said Henry. 'There's someone snooping about there, night after night, and since Pollitts put all those locks and chains over it I don't see how *anyone* could get in. Do you? So what's going on, and what are they after? That's what I'd like to know. Do you fancy coming?'

Nev wasn't listening. He was studying the eating away of the girl's left cheek very carefully and wondering if you could achieve the same effect with Blu-Tack. You could paint it red afterwards.

'You're not listening, are you?' Henry said huffily, getting up from the settee and pulling on his anorak. 'You say you're my best friend but you don't even listen when I speak to you. Some friend you are.'

Nev switched the video off completely. Henry *was* his best friend, the only loyal one, the only one who didn't tell tales about his absence notes or repeat funny stories about their daft family to Miss Bingham.

'*What* are you going on about?' he said, his mind still on the bees. '*Spring Mill?* We can't go back there, Henry, you know we can't. And *why* for heaven's sake? There's nothing there anyway.'

'I think there *is*,' Henry said stolidly. 'And I've explained once. Don't you ever listen? I've been back loads of times and I keep seeing this man on a motor bike. *He's* after something anyhow. He said he was the security guard, but he had the shock of his life when he saw me. He's interested in something anyhow, and I think it's his lights I keep seeing, from our attic.'

'Well *what*, for example?' Nev said. 'What *is* he after?'

Henry hesitated. This was the bit that sounded silly. 'I don't know, but I've a feeling it's connected with that raid on Schofield's shop, when they did the electrical place the same night. I mean, they could've used a place like Spring Mill for a base, couldn't they, they could've –'

'Oh, come off it, Henry. You've been watching too much crime on telly. In *Darnley*?'

Henry went to the door. Nev was a fine one to talk. He watched so much TV he'd got square eyes. He'd have a square head soon.

'Look, are you coming with me or not? We'll have to get in through the foundations because Pollitts have really given the place the third degree now, since winning the court case. There are supposed to be electric alarms, the lot. Will you come or not?'

'No,' said Nev. But he said it very quietly. It was great poking about the foundations of Spring Mill and it was hard, letting Henry down. He had been in a load of trouble with his dad recently and he'd get thrashed if they were found in there again. 'I'm sorry, Henry,' he said, 'but I just can't. You know what a foul temper my dad's got and he'd belt me. You can't make me risk that.'

Henry went off home without saying another word. Nev hadn't exactly said so but when he'd heard the theories about The Blob and Schofield's break-in the wide, half-baked expression that had crept across his face plainly said he thought his little friend was living in fairy-land.

Henry trudged home through a cold drizzle feeling lonely,

117

let-down, and bitterly disappointed. If Nev was chickening out then he really didn't have a friend in the world. Dad had simply disappeared. Where was he? In hospital? In prison? Every time he asked his mother she went all misty-eyed, and all Cousin Noreen did was to tell him to stop 'rabbiting on'. Life was just great.

At least all those cyclists were getting wet. There wasn't a soul between Nev's front door and their gate. Then he saw Desperate Dan, lolloping down towards the main road.

It was quite a shock seeing him again. He'd more or less gone to earth since that meeting under the holly bush, when Fred had roared up in his Lollocks van, and they'd only met once since, by the Jubilee Road dustbins one Tuesday night. Danny had started at one end and Henry at the other.

This time the old man ignored him completely. He clearly wasn't interested in Henry's doings any more, leg or no leg. There'd been nothing in the newspapers about the Schofield case, and no more pink faces peering in at his bedroom window. In fact if he'd not seen those lights again Henry really would have begun to think that he'd dreamed the whole thing up.

20

Then he saw The Blob again, down in the Covered Market. It was Saturday morning and he'd gone down to Whiteley's Cheese Stall for a pound of Lancashire. It was the best place for cheese in Darnley.

Noreen had sent him. She was still in bed, and so was his mother. He wouldn't normally have agreed to run errands for his cousin but she was doing most of the cooking these days. Henry loved food and mealtimes had become quite exciting. She needed the Lancashire cheese for a 'special Italian' dish. It didn't sound very Italian to Henry, but he got what she'd asked for. 'A pound of Lancashire, please,' he said to the woman. 'The mild one.'

After buying the cheese he went to see The Bulldog in the pet shop, to get a price for his pre-Christmas gerbils. But the man had obviously forgotten all about him and he wasn't very encouraging.

'There's a glut you see, son,' he said, weakly embarrassed.

'You said that last time,' Henry muttered through his teeth. It was rather rude but it was true, and anyway, where *were* all these gerbils? He could see rabbits and mice running round, and budgies in cages. But no gerbils.

He went off without getting the man to agree to anything. Perhaps he'd keep The Two Ronnies anyway; they'd improved since he'd separated them, and the little one had calmed down a bit. He quite liked the nibbling noises when he woke up in the middle of the night, especially now he felt that the rest of the world had let him down.

There was The Blob, at a record stall, sifting through Top of the Pops. He didn't look as if he'd washed his face or

changed his clothes since chasing Henry through the gates of
Spring Mill. His neck looked thicker, as if he'd put weight
on, and the greasy blonde hair was a few inches longer. But
it was definitely him.

Henry dodged behind a vegetable stall and lurked. At the
next rack a gangling teenager in jeans was looking at Brass
Band Selections. Henry peered through his spindly legs and
spied on The Blob.

He selected four records and paid for them in pound notes,
and there were more where those came from. He'd peeled
them off a roll that he'd pulled out of his back pocket. That
was fishy enough, but what Henry saw next was even more
fishy. The Blob was wearing three watches, not one, not two,
but *three*, two on the left arm and one on the right.

The blue jeans shifted at this point and Henry lost sight of
The Blob for a minute, but he saw the watches again, as a
sweaty pink hand leaned forward and grabbed some change
from the stall-holder. They were cheap and nasty watches,
the kind you see on special offer in filling-stations.

'Digital mainly, that's the stuff they go for . . .' Mr Schofield's words came back to him as The Blob went off towards the car park and left Henry propping up a heap of oranges by the vegetable stall. His brain was working overtime now. Could those three watches be left-overs from the break-in or was he simply going off his head?

He followed The Blob out of the Market and into the car park. From a safe distance he saw him rev up a motor bike and ride away. It was a different machine, good second-hand, not the rusty old one he'd seen at Spring Mill. The Blob was in the money now. Pity he didn't buy some new clothes.

Not for the first time Henry wished he was Superman, so he could sprout wings and follow him. In gangster films they'd have jumped in a taxi and shouted 'Follow That Motor Bike'.

Follow That Blob, Henry thought glumly as the bus crawled along Jubilee Road towards Fir Grove. Some hopes.

He put the cheese in the fridge and jammed a stool up against the door; otherwise it would swing open, and everything would go bad. Then he went upstairs to see Noreen. The iceberg music was turned up very loud, and the 'Do Not Disturb' notice was in position already. Apart from a spot of cooking she was planning to spend the whole weekend on her sculpt. Fred was banned till Sunday night.

When Henry knocked there was a scuffling noise. He waited quite patiently but he felt rather irritated. This thing she was making for the competition was taking over her life. Before anyone was allowed in she always threw a sheet over it. He could see it was big though, and getting bigger by the hour.

'How are you going to get it out of the house?' he asked curiously. All the entries had to be taken to the new Platt Art Centre behind the Town Hall. She'd need a crane if it got any bigger, or else they'd end up lowering it through the window on a winch.

'Oh, it dismantles,' she said airily, rearranging the sheet in case Henry started peeping. 'Fred's worked it out, it's quite ingenious.'

'Has he seen it then?' said Henry jealously. After all, she'd

121

only got the idea after seeing all his junk, and she kept on cadging things from him too. His Victorian attic was beginning to look quite bare.

'*No*,' Noreen replied emphatically, sounding rather shocked. 'Nobody's seen it, nobody at all, I've *told* you. I just showed Fred a diagram of it, and he's worked it out from that.'

'When can we see it then?'

'When it's on show. I've promised. If you see it before, Henry, it'll ruin it. I'll go off the boil and I won't be able to finish it. It's like poetry.'

Henry didn't understand but Noreen had that wild faraway look in her eyes again. She was still wearing her nightie and the draught-board hair with ginger patches was standing up on end. She must have been 'inspired' the minute she got out of bed. It wasn't the right moment to embark upon The Blob, which was what he'd come for.

'I'll go then,' he muttered. 'The cheese is in the fridge.'

'Thanks, Henry, you're a pal. Oh, and by the way . . .' She was scratching around for something to cheer him up; she was dying to get on with the 'sculpt' but not wanting to send him away in that mood. He looked dead miserable.

'By the way what?'

'Well, talking of poetry, I've sent in our entry for the Kelly Kitchen competition.'

'You've not!'

'Well of course I have. *You* wouldn't. Anything's worth a try.'

Henry went straight out, slamming the door behind him. There was a crash, and a wail from his cousin, but he didn't mind if he *had* wrecked her precious sculpture, which had presumably fallen over. He was absolutely furious.

She'd laughed her head off at his contribution to the couplet, and now she'd sent it in. It could only be because she thought they'd win a kind of booby prize.

He could remember their effort quite clearly:

Noreen: In the kitchen of life all good dreams start,
Henry: Six currant buns and a raspberry tart.

Well that was what people *made* in their kitchens, wasn't

it? It had quite a good ring to it. Henry had thought so anyway, until his mother and Noreen had started tittering.

He kicked savagely at his sag-bag. How could she *do* this to him? He had half a mind to go and ask for all his junk back. And then where would she be?

21

The weeks crawled by and they reached December. Christmas was coming, the season of goodwill and new bikes, but Henry wasn't looking forward to it at all. He'd spent last year's at Gran's, with his mother, and it was one big black memory. Never-ending telly, Mum's long face, and a turkey dinner that nobody wanted to eat, not even Henry.

It was wonderful timing, the final big row that had lasted all night, and his dad walking out on 22 December.

'Where is he now, Mum?' he said one night when Mrs Hooper seemed in rather a better mood than usual. She'd just got her Christmas bonus from the *Examiner*, along with everyone else. 'Kind of them, wasn't it?' she murmured, counting the pound notes. 'In view of the short time I've worked there.'

Not to mention all the late going in, Henry said to himself. But he kept his mouth buttoned up tight. It was important to keep his mother sweet-tempered if he was going to get any information about his father. 'Where is he?' he repeated. 'Have you seen him at all?'

She didn't answer this, but she did say he'd been on a mid-week trip to Paris with Uncle Bill.

'To *Paris*? In *this* weather?'

'That's what I said, to Paris. It was some special British Rail offer and they just took off. Had quite a nice time, I gather. You know your Uncle Bill and his wild schemes. It was for one of these books he's supposed to be writing.'

So she had seen him then. Henry was sure of it. And he must be feeling better too. If he was still ill he'd not have risked eating frogs' legs and stuff, would he?

'And is he still at Uncle Bill's?'

Mrs Hooper shrugged. 'I don't know, chick. The town flat's still being paid for, but there's never anyone in. Anyway you might – look, love, he might drop in before Christmas, so let's wait and see, shall we?'

It must be all this contact with Cousin Noreen that was doing it. *Wait and see.* Grandma Clegg made wait-and-see pudding, though it was always exactly the same – stewed apple with soggy meringue on top. Was it his imagination or did Mrs Hooper seem slightly more cheerful?

It was probably the money. She was already looking in the newspapers to see when the January sales started.

According to Cousin Noreen there were definite 'negotiations' going on. She was getting ready to deliver her 'sculpt' and when she wasn't at the Poly she was shut away in her attic, working on it. She still kept her eyes skinned for people coming up the drive though. Desperate Dan's secret visit to steal the leg had made her nervous, and Fred had fixed a lock on her door. She told Henry that his father had visited one Wednesday, on his mother's afternoon off, and that there'd been somebody with him.

'Who?' Henry wanted to know. How could his father come back after all this time and not wait till he came home? It was awful of him.

'Someone official-looking,' said Noreen. 'A man in a suit.'

'Oh, it'd be a solicitor,' Henry said darkly. 'It'd be about money,' and his hopes sagged again, like undercooked Yorkshire puddings.

Money may not make you happy, but perhaps it makes being miserable easier to bear. 'Fabulous, Henry, really original,' Miss Bingham had twittered on when she read his composition, 'Only, well, dear, you don't really reach any *conclusion* do you? What else could you say?'

Only that his mum and dad had had their biggest argument ever three days before Christmas last year, and that nothing had gone right since. But it was too personal. He wasn't having that read out in class.

The Kelly Kitchen competition was won by a woman in Oldham. Noreen and Henry read the report in the *Examiner* and agreed that she was a professional. Last year she'd won a holiday for two in the Bahamas, off a cornflakes packet, and her own kitchen looked pretty dream-like already. The newspaper had photographed her standing by a split-level oven grinning like a maniac and waving her winning couplet at the camera.

'Note that they didn't *print* her poem, Hen,' Noreen said suspiciously. 'I bet it was fixed.'

'I'm glad they didn't print ours,' he muttered, looking fearfully at the report. It had taken him a long time to forgive her for sending it off without telling him. 'And *don't call me Hen.*' Privately though, he'd decided she really couldn't help it – she was so absorbed in her creation up in the attic that she was on Cloud Nine most of the time. Sometimes she just didn't seem to know what she was saying.

'Will you get any money if you win your art competition?' he asked her. 'Or is it just for the glory?' It'd be good if someone at Fir Grove made a bit of cash, and he obviously wasn't going to.

'Oh, you just get the glory,' Cousin Noreen said solemnly. 'But it's the winning that counts, Hen.'

'Really?' Henry grunted as he went off to school. He wasn't so sure about that.

Mavis Bramley was up in arms about the woman from Oldham. Another local newspaper had said rather more about her. She'd not only won the cornflakes holiday but she was a regular winner at the Bingo Hall, and she'd once had some fat pickings on Premium Bonds. Mavis wasn't Henry's favourite person – she was a bit too loud and bossy for him – but he felt quite sympathetic as she raved on about the Kelly Competition. 'People like that should have been *excluded,*' she argued loudly, and he did agree. It was a swizz really.

Miss Bingham suggested they might write to Kelly Kitchens and complain about the rules. Mavis agreed to think about it, and told Henry she was going to consult her dad. 'It's no good, Mavis,' Henry told her at dinner time, when she was still ranting on about the unfairness of it all. 'There's no justice, you know, and people don't listen to children.'

*

And it was because nobody would listen to him, or co-operate, or answer any of his questions, that Henry had gone 'underground' in his criminal investigations. He'd secretly read all the papers he could lay his hands on, to find out more about the Schofield affair, but it wasn't in any of them.

Local newspapers were pathetic anyway, and the *Darnley Examiner* was the worst of the lot. No wonder Mrs Hooper was getting tired of her new job. 'Thieves broke into 17 King Street, the home of Mr and Mrs Arnold Haggerty, on Tuesday night, and stole a hair-drier worth £3.50 and a tin of tongue.' The *Examiner*'s circulation was dropping, and if that was their idea of front-page news they deserved it. Henry had abandoned it long ago in his search for clues.

His mother did let one thing out though, in an unguarded moment. It was about the stuff for 'valuation' that had gone missing. 'I honestly don't know what it was,' she muttered vaguely, 'but it was obviously worth a packet because it belonged to old Miss Templeton up on Bradshaw Drive. That house is like Aladdin's Cave.'

'Not *her*, Mum,' said Henry, 'not *Edith* Templeton. She's a real old bat, she is. Remember that time Nev and I went along Bradshaw Drive collecting pennies for the guy? She threw a wellington at us.'

'Bet it was an old one,' Mrs Hooper said, grinning. 'She's fabulously rich, even richer now the sister's died. I liked May a lot better. Everyone did. But this one's a real shark when it comes to money, and she's determined to get what she can out of poor old Nellie Schofield. The fact that her husband's only just died doesn't seem to enter into it at all. She's as hard as nails.

'She's always sending letters to the editor as well. There's always something wrong on Bradshaw Drive – drains, bad street lights, vandalism. She's a real frost that woman.'

Henry was getting quite hopeful. Perhaps if he just sat quietly and waited he might get the whole story, Spring Mill and everything.

But his mother knew the expression in his eyes too well. 'I should have kept my trap shut, you know,' she said hurriedly. 'Even to you. The police've already been to see us twice and I bet they'll be round again if Nellie doesn't pay up. So *Mum's the word*. OK!'

'Yes, Mum,' said Henry. He knew he'd had his money's worth anyway. She'd got a large piece of paper out and was busy listing all the after-Christmas sales.

Later he told Noreen what she'd said. She knew all about Edith Templeton, from Grandma Clegg. Mum was dead right apparently, the house on Bradshaw Drive *was* full of treasures. The father, old Dr Templeton, had been a great collector, mainly of things from the East. Now he was dead, and poor, gentle May was dead too, it all belonged to Battleaxe Edith and it was something from the collection that had gone to Mr Schofield for valuation.

'I wonder what it was though?' said Henry. 'And if it was so priceless why didn't she take it to one of the big jewellers in Manchester? Or to London even? Why go to Schofield's?'

'Because she's mean, I should think. Rich people very often are, that's how they make their money. You have to *pay*, Hen, to get things valued. I suppose she wanted it done on the cheap.'

'And the burglars nicked it,' Henry said thoughtfully.

'Serve her right, I think, she's a real tartar. And now she's trying to get the money out of old Mrs Schofield, poor old thing.'

But Arthur Schofield's widow wasn't a poor thing at all; she was a fighter. Henry met her one Sunday afternoon at his gran's, sitting on the settee with a cup of tea and a barm cake, a little round woman with coal-black eyes. She reminded him of a currant bun.

They were talking about Edith Templeton and the money when Henry walked in. They stopped when they saw him, but he did hear that Mrs Schofield wasn't going to pay up without a struggle. 'It's the least I can do for Arthur,' she was saying bravely, as he came down the hall. 'And the reward's still on offer, that might do something.'

Henry still believed that the answer lay with The Blob and Spring Mill. Every night, before he settled down on his mattress, he spent a few minutes at the window just to make sure there was nothing going on. But there never was, and The Blob never went back to that record stall. Henry walked down to the Covered Market several times afterwards, and hung round in the car park. But The Blob did not return.

Christmas was in the air, and Miss Bingham's band were practising Six Little Carols in the dinner hour. It had shrunk considerably over the weeks and it now consisted of three triangles, one violin and the golden flute of Jonathan Pargetter. The repair bill had come through Henry's letter box along with some Christmas cards. That was another reason for not mentioning a new bike.

The three Hodgkinsons needed money for presents so they went round the estate. Nev did a nice line in carols but he never knew when to stop, The Ugly Sisters egged him on. Noreen heard them through her attic window, bellowing outside Snells'.

> 'Hark the herald angels sing,
>   Beecham's Pills are just the thing.
>   Peace on earth and mercy mild,
>   Two for adults and one for a child.'

Fortunately, Mrs Snell was out at a Women's Institute meeting, but Graham's dad heard them. He gave them 10p each and told them to go and sing outside their own front gate.

Mr Hooper, well or ill, or just in Paris, seemed to have gone into hiding. Henry had been back twice to the town flats but number 12C was still all locked up, and there was the same scene of desolation through the keyhole, the piles of washing, the unwashed cups, and the same red and white shirt dangling over the chair back.

He really felt he could insist on being told the facts but Mrs Hooper had gone into one of her big depressions, and you had to be very careful when she was in this mood.

In any case, Henry wasn't sure she actually *knew* the facts. Dad was apparently shacked up somewhere with Uncle Bill, according to Grandma Clegg, and that could mean anywhere, from Land's End to John O'Groats. The caravan was too cold to live in during the winter.

If she didn't resign from the *Examiner* they would probably sack her anyway. She went into the office later and later, and sometimes she didn't go at all. She said the hours were too long, the pay too low, and that it was slave labour in spite of the December bonus.

The glamour of a new job never lasted long these days, but it hadn't always been like that. She was falling apart without Dad.

Even The Blob had Christmas presents to buy because the week before the 25th Henry got another sighting. It was down in the Covered Market again.

He hadn't actually gone Blob-spotting, he'd gone down to find out the price of Christmas trees. Noreen was organizing the Hoopers' celebrations before she went home to Harrogate, and she was determined to do it properly. 'A little tree and all the trimmings, Hen, you both need cheering up, I think. It's my Christmas present; it's great living with you and your mum,' she'd told him.

So Henry had been dispatched to the Market to see if there were any great bargains. There weren't any but there was The Blob, spending money as if it had just come into fashion – boxes of cigarettes, booze, fancy after-shave and half a dozen records from the stall Henry had watched so often, from his post by the oranges.

His face hadn't improved; it was more pimply than ever, and a lot fleshier. He was obviously getting fat on his pickings, whatever his game was. And his clothes were new too, a denim suit with very tight trousers and pointed boots. Eunice Snell would have loved him.

When he walked off towards the car park Henry didn't bother following. He couldn't very well go up to him and accuse him of giving old Mr Schofield a fatal heart attack. But on the bus ride home he resolved to do one thing. He'd keep up his watch on the mill till Christmas, and if he saw anything he'd definitely go and investigate on his own.

If he didn't make himself do it he'd never get to the bottom of the Schofield affair, or the mystery of the leg, and he owed it to himself. Like Noreen, Henry had Grandfather Clegg's blood in his veins, and when Cleggs got their teeth into something they didn't let go easily.

22

A few days later something woke him up at two in the morning, but this time it wasn't a face at the window, it was a little chewing noise. Big Ronnie was up and about and having a midnight feast. Henry wouldn't have woken up normally, but he couldn't sleep properly these days. He had too much on his mind.

He got up from his mattress, crept across the floor, and looked out. It was a mild, almost muggy night, unusual for mid December. Noreen was hoping for a white Christmas but she was going to be disappointed. She'd got white on the brain.

He spent ages at the window, staring hard and seeing nothing. He was thinking of his father, and of his mother's misery, and of happier Christmasses all together at Fir Grove. So when he saw the light in Spring Mill he didn't take much notice at first. He thought he'd been dreaming.

There were murky, fuzzy lights all over Darnley, strings of them slung along the motorway like big orange beads, and twinkling house lights like the points of pins. There were lamps along the canal bank now as well; they'd gone up in November. The Council was trying to make it into an 'urban conservation area' even though it was one of the most polluted waterways in Lancashire.

He started to get his stuff together but he still wasn't sure. He *had* seen a light, twice in five minutes, but it was all so muddled on a night like this. It could have been car lights coming down off the dual carriageway, or the flashing of a police car or an ambulance.

Big Ronnie was having a thoroughly good chew and

watching him from the corner of his cage. *Yes*, Henry thought sourly, pushing a torch into his anorak pocket and looking round for his bobble hat. If it hadn't been for you, mate, I might still be asleep. Two minutes later though, he was creeping through the back door, bike lamp in hand, to get to his fairy-cycle, with the great hump of the sleeping house looming over him like a giant. He felt a bit scared.

In places the towpath was slippy with mud and Henry pedalled precariously, dodging the puddles. The canal bank was totally deserted and he was soon leaning his bike against the mossy mill wall. One of the new lamps was quite near his hole so he didn't need his torch immediately. He bent down and began hacking at the brambles.

He only had a rusty old clasp knife so it took a long time, and his hands were soon scratched and bleeding. But at last the tangle of spiky branches could be pulled right back, and there was the hole, inviting him in.

The smell coming out of it was anything but inviting – it was cheese and old socks and lavatories all mixed up – and it looked so small, even smaller than when he'd examined it weeks ago, way back in October. There'd only just been room to wriggle through last summer and he'd grown a bomb since then. What if he got stuck half-way in, like Winnie the Pooh? Gran used to read him those stories.

Henry put his knife away and remounted his fairy-cycle. There was no harm in going round to the mill gates for a minute, just to see if the padlocks were off again. Anything rather than go down into the foundations through that hole, all on his own. If he was right, and somebody *was* in the mill, they must have got through the Pollitt security system, so why couldn't he follow them in?

At two o'clock on a winter's morning Spring Mill looked terrifying. There was nobody about but Henry didn't go up to the gates, not yet. He couldn't. Instead he hovered by the crumbling wall in the long grass, where he'd spied on the men from Pollitt's Estates, staring at the ravaged buildings behind their wreaths of barbed wire, feeling the sadness of it all.

The empty mill was like an abandoned ship or an old machine chucked on the scrap-heap because it was no use any more. But it was ghostly too, and as he stared up at it the high buildings seemed to grow higher, as if they were gathering themselves up to come and get him.

Henry tried to pull himself together. He got his torch out of his pocket and flashed it over the gates. Everything seemed to be in position as before, and the whole place was in darkness, but he wasn't giving up, not yet. He crouched in the long grass, with the wet seeping up through the seat of his pants, shining his torch along the mill walls, then back to the huge gates again, his ears pricked for the tiniest noise.

And in the end he heard something, a muffled thump that came from somewhere in the shadows on the far side of the mill yard, a door being pulled shut.

He got up and stole across the grass. The thumping noise came again, and again, but each time it was fainter, as if whoever was in there was working his way through a series of little rooms. That could be right too; there'd be a whole warren of them inside a place like Spring Mill, rooms for this and rooms for that, rooms underneath too. At one point Grandma Clegg had been a 'winder' and she'd worked in a cellar all day.

He was close to the gates now, and he looked at them carefully. The three new padlocks were undone, and there was an eighteen-inch gap. Someone had obviously picked them, and squeezed through.

But Henry remained cautious. He flashed his torch up on to the walls and had another look at the barbed wire. Threaded through it was a thin red cable. It ran along the left-hand wall from end to end, snaked down through one of the gates, through the rusty ironwork, and disappeared into the rubble of the mill yard.

It must work some kind of alarm. Whoever was in there hadn't spotted it, or else had been plain lucky. But Henry wasn't taking any chances. He could just see it; he'd be half-way across the yard and alarms would start ringing, and he'd end up with some bullying police officer carting him away in a Black Maria. It'd be safer to risk getting stuck in that hole. So he went back and had another look at it.

As it turned out he got through quite easily, so he couldn't have put on too much weight since last year. The cheesy old-socks smell was much stronger inside, and Henry put one hand over his nose as he wriggled forwards, otherwise he might be sick.

He'd already switched his torch on, but it wasn't much use. The dark inside the foundations was wrapped all round him like a thick, black cloth and he worked by feel, rather than by using his eyes. He was crawling downwards, making his way right across the mill under the main cellars. They'd never got more than half-way across before, they'd been too scared. But Nev reckoned you'd reach a flight of steps if you went far enough, and a door that took you into the mill itself. Their Art had been in once.

The smell got steadily worse. Henry kept banging into the wooden props that held up the mill floor; it was like being in a coal-mine. Then something ran over his foot. *Ugh.* He gave a little squeal and dropped his torch. He was getting out of this place quick. He was already being suffocated and now there were rats waiting to eat him. Why had he ever come down here? He must be off his head.

Then, somewhere up above, he heard a shuffling noise and someone coughed. Henry froze and scrabbled round in the blackness, his shaking fingers feeling for the torch. After that squeal he didn't dare switch it back on. In the enormous silence of the abandoned mill the least noise sounded like an explosion.

So he stayed exactly where he was, rigid with nerves and with the back of his neck all prickly, listening as the muffled footsteps died away and yet another door thumped shut.

His torch was still working, which was something, and when he flashed it around, trying to get his bearings, he saw the flight of steps. Clever old Art. There it was, only inches away from his nose, and a great yawning hole at the top where a door had been wrenched off.

Henry worked his way upwards, his ears throbbing with nerves. It took him a long time because every few seconds he stopped and listened, just in case the footsteps came back. But the silence was total, broken only by his quick nervous breathing, and the thumpity-thump of his own heart.

At the top of the steps he went through the empty doorway into a great room, windowless and bare apart from some huge iron brackets in the floor from which, presumably, all the old machinery had long since been ripped away. Perhaps it was the 'winding room'. Fancy Grandma Clegg working in a place like this.

There were three more rooms and Henry crept through them, shining his torch carefully round. There was nothing in them at all apart from dust and bricks. The only thing alive was the brooding darkness, full of horrors and spiders, waiting to pounce.

It was the fifth room that showed signs of occupation. There were steps leading out of it and at the top a door three quarters shut. That staircase must take you up into the ground floor of the mill eventually, but he wasn't investigating further, not just yet anyway.

It was obvious that a lot of people had been down here, perhaps even camped out. He could see heaps of old mattresses and moth-eaten pillows, pieces of blanket and used-up candles stuck in jam jars. There were dozens of empty tins too, soup and baked beans, all mixed together with dozens of mouldy bread wrappers. And heaped up in one corner, almost touching the ceiling, was a huge pile of junk. His kind.

With the help of his now wavering torch Henry ran his professional eye over it. It seemed to consist of packaging mainly, blocks of polystyrene and plastic bags, dozens of small cartons that had once contained radios and cassette recorders. Graham Snell could have made a really big railway layout with that lot.

Right at the bottom of the heap he found some really incriminating evidence, hundreds of little boxes, all flattened by someone's big feet. They were watch boxes, cheap and nasty, the kind sold in filling-stations.

Henry took a step back and considered. There was no doubt about it, he'd stumbled on a modern 'robbers' hoard', the place where they'd all gathered to go through their pickings, strip the wrappers off, and work out how to get rid of the stuff for ready cash. Some 'hoard' though, about three tons of empty cardboard boxes. Henry was disgusted.

It was only by chance he saw the foot. A faint, faraway noise somewhere over his head had made him jump and he'd turned away from the rubbish pile to get his bearings, just in case he had to make a dash for it, back to the hole. It was definitely a foot; the heel was now sticking out from all the cardboard boxes. He must have uncovered it himself. It looked just as though someone had been in the act of running away and got suddenly flattened by a crane-load of polystyrene waste.

Henry got hold of the foot and tugged. The mountain of cardboard and plastic bags disintegrated and everything fell apart in clouds of dust. In the silence the noise sounded like a small earthquake but he paid no attention to it. He was much too busy concentrating on what he'd just pulled out of the junk heap. It was a pink plastic leg. *His leg*.

But how could it be? That leg was in two pieces and

covered in paint and plaster up in Noreen's attic. It had become part of a great work of art, or so she was always telling him. Henry couldn't make head or tail of it; all this crawling about in acres of smelly darkness was obviously affecting his brain.

But if it wasn't *his* leg who the heck's was it?

'Mine I think,' said a voice, obviously reading his thoughts. 'You've saved me quite a job finding that. I've been trying to get in here for weeks, to go over the place, but I was always being disturbed by little visitors. First Pollitt's lot, then Platt's, snooping around. They're a right shower. Not much to choose between them, I'd say. They never found *me*.'

The voice belched and the petrified Henry smelt beer. It was a fat voice, fat like its owner. 'Hand it over, sunshine,' it went on, 'hand it over like a good lad and I'll let you go.'

But the voice had an unpleasant sneer in it. Its owner didn't look too pleasant either, and it was standing at the top of the stone staircase, staring down at Henry with its arms folded. It was The Blob.

23

What happened next happened in total silence. It was uncanny. The Blob and Henry followed each other round and round that airless room, like two rival gangsters in a midnight movie, with the sound switched off. Henry kept tight hold of the leg, and he held on to his torch too. It'd be fatal to drop it in a place like this.

His mother had accidentally switched the light off once, when he'd been rooting about in their own cellar, under Fir Grove, and he'd stumbled about in the dark for ages before she'd heard him yelling. If you lost your bearings down here you might never get out.

Perhaps The Blob had been locked in a cellar too, in his youth. He was carrying a large flash-light and he kept firm hold of it, so there was only one fat arm left to grab Henry and the leg. It shouldn't be much of a fight; the boy was big for his age but The Blob must weigh about fourteen stone.

Henry was much nimbler though, and obviously thought quicker. He danced about round the man's feet, trying to get to the steps, but always slithering out of reach when the arm came too near him. Then he switched his own torch off. Now The Blob'd have to go hunting for him. With luck he could slip through his legs, get up the stairs, then off through the yard and away.

When the torch went out the man started swearing, then he fell over something and Henry heard a series of grunts. Come to think of it, he'd only heard The Blob speak once before, weeks ago out in the mill yard, when he'd pretended to be the Securicor man. Perhaps this man was like Danny

Crompton and only spoke when strictly necessary. Perhaps it was the criminal temperament.

For a minute everything went dead quiet and Henry began to panic. He couldn't even hear The Blob breathing now, and yet he must be very close. It was unnerving. Still clutching the leg he flicked his own little torch back on again and stared wildly round. It was the worse moment of all. He found himself standing in a corner by the cardboard rubbish heap with The Blob in spitting distance, towering over him like Dracula, with a horrible grin on his face.

Henry whipped round, charged up the staircase and squeezed through the rotting door, stopping for a split second to try and close it, to give himself more time. But with a roar The Blob at once hurtled off in pursuit, up the steps and out into a great empty hall with a high echoing roof. It felt as big as a church and at the far end Henry's fading yellow beam picked out an open door.

He ran forward, holding his torch out straight in front of him, like the very last runner in some crazy relay race. He was concentrating on that door, and his feet, and not dropping the leg. The Blob puffed behind him, swearing horribly between grunts, through the door, down a narrow dark passageway to another door, across the rutted yard to the gates.

Henry daren't stop to examine that red cable though he'd seen it quite clearly, sneaking through a clump of shrivelled grass and squeezing itself under a slab of concrete. He didn't need to open the gates any wider anyway; The Blob must have squeezed through the gap and so could he.

But one of them must have touched something vital because, as he tore round the corner of the outer mill wall, and back on to the canal bank, it sounded as if all the burglar alarms in Darnley had started ringing at once.

The mud on the towpath was slowing Henry down. On a crisp dry night he'd have covered that half-mile quite quickly – he'd raced it many a time with Nev, down to the Rec. Now he kept slipping in the sticky puddles, then he dropped his torch, and when he turned round he saw that The Blob was gaining on him fast.

The boy pelted on but his head was swimming strangely. He didn't know if he was asleep or awake, or just slowly dying. It was as if he'd passed out of reality and gone into a kind of fantasy world where a big beery monster was chasing him along a bank, and he was carrying part of a body all in pieces, and there were bells in his ears that just wouldn't stop ringing.

He was going to be sick and it felt as if all the blood in his chest was coming up through his windpipe, squeezing up painfully, trying to choke him to death. Now he was falling forward slowly, and a great patch of oily mud gleamed wetly under his tottering feet like a big black banana skin. He turned round for the last time and saw The Blob's face, swollen dark pink with rage and a big sloppy mouth in the middle, gibbering soundlessly at him. He turned, ran forward, slipped, and went straight into the canal.

'I'm drowning,' thought Henry as the water closed over his head. 'This is what dying's like.' He couldn't swim anyway, so he couldn't do much. Wasn't he supposed to thrash around though, to stop himself developing hypothermia? Or tread water? He'd never mastered that, nor the art of the back-leg frog kick. His best hope was for a friendly branch to come floating by, so he could grab hold of it.

It was as if time had stopped altogether. Perhaps it was the shock of the freezing canal, or all the water he'd swallowed. He felt curiously peaceful. Perhaps he would see his eleven years of life flash by, like people said. An old drunk had drowned in the canal only last week. Did it take longer, if you were old?

But The Blob was in the water too and he'd seized him under the armpits. 'Stick your legs out, you silly little fool,' he bellowed through mouthfuls of weed. 'Stick your legs out, or you'll go under. And put your head back . . . no, like *that*. Do you want to drown us both?'

Henry forgot everything afterwards, except the wobbling white moon reflected in the slimy black water, and the indescribable smell of the canal. He saw the leg too, as it floated peacefully away towards the Rec. If he died he would

141

never know its secret, or what it had contained. The winning couplet in the Kitchen Competition? An instant cure for freckles? He was still thinking about it as The Blob lugged him up on to the bank, and he passed out.

24

Henry wasn't well after that; in fact he was quite ill and he missed Christmas. Mrs Hooper was puzzled. The boy was as strong as a horse and she thought he'd recover in no time from his midnight dip in the Darnley Canal. But he didn't. First he developed a raging temperature, then he became delirious and couldn't recognize people. In the end she had to call the doctor out in the middle of the night.

He kept coming to see him too, all over Christmas. Mrs Hooper sat in the attic morning, noon and night, and their presents lay unopened under Noreen's artistic tree. She kept phoning up from Harrogate and his dad came too, several times in the first few days. Well, Mum said he'd been. Henry couldn't remember.

The first visitor he recognized was Eunice Snell. She came panting up the attic stairs with a box of Dairy Milk and a book of educational animal photographs, and she sat right on the edge of his sag-bag, as if it was diseased.

But she was quite kind to Henry, and very concerned about the 'accident'. She blamed everything on the canal water, well, he'd swallowed enough of it. 'It's filthy,' she told Mrs Hooper fiercely. 'They should fill that canal in, not make it into a park. We ought to write to the council about it.'

The three Hodgkinsons came too, giggling and dumping a load of old Beanos on his mattress, and Miss Bingham breezed up one day after school, with a big 'Get Well' card signed by the whole class. She thought his attic bedroom was absolutely fabulous.

But it wasn't till Noreen came back, in January, that Henry found out what he really wanted to know. He'd not really asked before – he'd felt too ill – and his mother hadn't brought the subject up either yet; she'd been too worried about him.

Cousin Noreen had been keeping her ears wide open as usual, and she told him what she'd managed to find out. The Blob had rescued him from the canal – well, they all knew that. It was either the leg or Henry, and the boy couldn't really have been left to drown, not even by Duggie James, which was The Blob's real name.

In gratitude for his heroic efforts over Henry the police had apprehended Duggie on the towpath. Between them, in their flight from the mill, they'd set all the alarm bells ringing at the local sub-station. Old Man Pollitt never did things by halves, and after winning his court case he'd done the protection bit properly, with no expenses spared. Two officers had been on the scene in no time, just as Duggie was trying to get Henry up on to his feet.

'What about the leg though?' said Henry. 'Did they find it?' He supposed he ought to be grateful to The Blob, but this was the important issue.

'No,' Noreen said blankly. 'I suppose it sank.'

'But it was *floating*,' Henry muttered, in a puzzled voice. 'I saw it. It was going down towards the Rec.'

'Well perhaps it filled with water,' said Cousin Noreen. 'I mean, if you fill a tin can up it sinks, and that's hollow.'

'So it *wasn't* your leg then, the one you used for the sculpt?'

She looked at him, wide-eyed beneath her fuzz of ginger hair. 'Well, *no*, Hen, how could it be?' She was slightly puzzled. He was supposed to be on the mend but all this about that leg was worrying her. Perhaps his brain was still a bit pickled in canal water.

'Who's The Blob then?'

'The *Blob*?'

'That man who fished me out of the canal. Is he in prison?'

'No, not that I've heard. I've told you, his name's Duggie James; he's been in trouble with the police loads of times, he was in a big gang originally. He's being a good boy now though, he's "helping the police with their inquiries". He's got "friends" you see, and the police want to know about all them, now the old gang's split up and disappeared.'

'I knew they were a bunch of thieves,' Henry said, lying

back on his pillows. 'There was loads of stuff at Spring Mill, well empty boxes. They were lucky nobody had got through to that room before, I think. They'd been sort of squatting in it, primus stoves and everything. They must have been flogging it somewhere pretty regularly. I bet they were the ones who broke into Schofield's. And I saw The Blob in the Market, wearing *three* watches. He can't be very bright can he, drawing attention to himself like that? And he had stacks of pound notes, Noreen.'

She glanced at him, still white and worried-looking on his mattress. His great crop of freckles had become the palest smudges now.

'Any news of Dad?' he whispered, as she turned to go into her own room.

She looked back. 'Not much, but you know he's been ill, don't you? He got a really bad virus and was off work for weeks, and it left him feeling very depressed, I gather. This is all from Gran so *keep your mouth shut*. He went off with your Uncle Bill eventually, to "have a good old think about everything"; well, that's what Gran said.'

'And what about Sheila Howarth?'

'Who? Oh, *her*. New boyfriend, I gather, someone in Bingley that sells computers or something.'

So she was off the scene at last. Did Mum know? She *must*.

'Noreen I want . . . I want . . .' It was awful, but he felt he was going to cry.

'Be *patient*, Hen. Get better first. He came to see you when you were ill, you know. He'll be back. Meanwhile, I'd get ready for a little visit from the police if I were you. You've been working out quite a lot, haven't you, considering you're supposed to be at death's door? I should think they'll be round any day now. Get your story lined up, Hen,' she added wickedly.

Henry went very quiet after that and lay nervously waiting for the phone to ring, or for another great hammering on the front door. He might be in trouble too, along with Duggie James. He *had* gone into Spring Mill after all, *broken* in really, and it *was* private property.

The police did come and Mum sat with him, on guard like a mother hen with a great overgrown chick. They asked quite

145

a few questions, about what had happened down in the mill cellars, and what he'd seen. But they were very gentle with him really, and went away telling him not to worry about a thing.

Nothing very interesting happened until the leg was found, and that wasn't until the canal had thawed out and somebody could go down. There'd been a sudden cold snap immediately after Christmas, and everything had frozen over.

If it hadn't been for old Nellie Schofield the leg wouldn't have been rescued at all, but she was a fighter, and determined to clear her husband's name. She wasn't giving in to Edith Templeton's ridiculous demands for money either. She'd been told about The Blob's capers with Henry at Spring Mill, and she knew the police had found evidence that Duggie and 'friends' had broken into Schofield's shop, and also raided the electrical store next door.

The young crooks weren't his 'friends' any more apparently, as Noreen had explained to Henry. He'd quarrelled with them, and formed a splinter group of one. But he did know that the missing leg was important for reasons that the police were keeping quiet, and that was why he'd kept trying to get into Spring Mill, to find it.

So now three people believed in the leg – Henry, The Blob and old Nellie Schofield. Noreen said she was keeping an open mind on the subject.

25

Soon after New Year a police frogman went diving in the Darnley Canal, just below the Rec. He came up with an old bicycle, half a pram and Henry's other leg. It was taken to the police station and described in minute detail in an official report: 'Right-hand leg from female fashion dummy, pink, plastic, 31½ inches long.' And the maker's name was stamped round the top in little letters. 'Made by Goldsworthy's of Manchester for Alice Modes Fashions, Accrington, Rochdale and Darnley.'

So that was one bit of the mystery solved. On the Tuesday night, when the staff of Alice Modes had put out their bins and gone home, there'd obviously been two plastic legs in Jubilee Road.

Mrs Ellis, the manageress, had just taken on a school-leaver who'd been causing her problems, on and off, for months. His main employment was to carry messages between the three shops on his motor scooter, but he was a kind of odd-job man too. And *he'd* thrown that rubbish out. Before doing so though, he'd had a mad five minutes in the back room with a little saw, hacking the unwanted model to pieces before putting it out with the bins. The dismembered leg sticking straight out of the rubbish was clearly his idea of a joke.

Mrs Ellis had given him his notice since. She said he'd caused more trouble than he realized, and that he should stop watching so many horror films, and go to bed at night.

Thanks to him there'd been two discarded legs outside the shop, while Henry sat in the cinema. There might have been hands in the gutter and heads rolling about under the lamplight too. Who would ever know, and what did it matter now? What mattered was that one of the legs had been used by the gang in a moment of panic.

They'd obviously broken into the electrical shop, and then into Schofield's, but something, some noise perhaps, must have disturbed them while they were still in there, and unnerved them. Inside the jeweller's they'd stuffed what they could into their pockets, digital clocks and watches, pen alarms, cheap things they could sell very easily, in large numbers.

But one of the gang was greedy. He'd seen something rather more promising than digital watches under Mr Schofield's work bench, something in a small bag. He must have snatched it up, run with it, and eventually, when the bikes and the old van had skidded into the dustbins, all in a heap outside Alice Modes, he'd rammed it down the leg, knowing that it could go on the van and end up in Spring Mill with all the electrical goods, and watches. He must have been planning to remove it privately, later on, and make a packet out of it.

But Mr Greedy, whoever it was, hadn't reckoned with the break-up of the gang. All the sudden police activity scared the pants off him, and he'd left Darnley in quite a hurry; so had most of his cronies. In any case, Spring Mill had been made 'secure' again only days after the two robberies so there was no chance of his getting the leg back anyway.

And it might never have been seen again if Henry hadn't gone into action, that week before Christmas.

Perhaps Mr Greedy might have hung around longer, if he'd known what it contained, but he wasn't the only one to make a fatal mistake that night. It was a right leg, not a left. That's where Desperate Dan, spying on the proceedings from a safe, dark alley, had got it wrong. All those consultations under lampposts, and bargainings with The Blob, all that effort to get up to Henry's attic with his wooden peg dragging, and then it was the *wrong leg*. He could have murdered him.

To get the mystery item out intact the leg had to be sawn in two, like Henry's. It was done in the police station, with everyone looking on, and the operation was quite delicate.

148

There, stuck in the ankle, was a small wash-leather bag and inside it were some small pieces of carved stone, orange and green, semi-transparent, like big wine gums, but carved with the patterns of animals and birds, and with fantastic dragons. They didn't weigh more than a few ounces.

It was jade, Chinese jade, extremely old and extremely rare. Worth a packet. Miss Templeton's father had been an oriental expert, and it had been his. Henry stuck loyally to Mr Schofield to the very end. He must have thought the bag contained jewellery – how could an old watchmender in Darnley be expected to get antique jewellery valued? She deserved what had happened because of her meanness in not going to a proper valuer, and she was luckier than she knew in getting it back at all.

Henry never actually saw it himself; it went straight into the bank and never saw the light of day again. But Noreen showed him some very like it, in a glass case in the Municipal Art Gallery and Museum. It looked boring to him.

'I just can't understand anyone collecting that,' he whispered, but very quietly because there was a ferret-faced official around, the sort who behaved as if everything in the place belonged to him personally, and you were out to steal it.

'Oh, it's old, Hen, old and very rare,' she told him dreamily. 'You're looking at history now; look at that dragon, look at its tail. Done on a thumb-nail almost. Don't you see?'

He listened politely, but he didn't really understand. It was funny what people paid good money for. This stuff for example, Noreen said it was worth thousands. And to think he'd nearly been drowned, for that.

'So Miss Templeton's got her jade back and Nellie Schofield doesn't have to pay up,' Noreen remarked afterwards, as they went to look for Fred's van in the town centre car park. He wasn't interested in jade either. He was in Darnley getting a drum mended.

And Mr Schofield's dead, Henry thought sadly, and that's that.

But it wasn't quite. Two days later a letter came for Henry in the post. It was a Saturday morning and he was just thinking about getting up. Noreen tore in with it and sat on the sag-bag while he read it through. She was very interested in other people's mail.

Nellie Schofield's writing was rather wobbly and hard to decipher, and the letter was full of 'heart-felt thanks' and 'deepest gratitude'.

'Gorgeous handwriting,' murmured Noreen, unashamedly reading it over his shoulder. 'Proper copperplate that is. Wish I could do it.'

But Henry wasn't looking at old Nellie's gorgeous copperplate script. All he saw was the cheque.

'It's the reward, it's the *reward*!' Noreen yelled, grabbing it and thumping him so hard on the back he nearly choked. '*Two hundred pounds*, Hen, now that's worth having. It was worth swallowing a bit of canal water for that. It's *fantastic*, Henry!' And she gave him a big sloppy kiss. He was so shocked he didn't mind for once.

Not only shocked but stunned. *Two hundred pounds for*

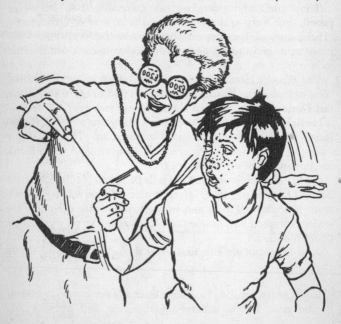

information leading to the recovery of Miss Templeton's jade. He wasn't sure he deserved it really; it didn't seem quite fair on The Blob somehow, especially not after that rescue from Darnley Canal. He'd been after the reward obviously, along with Desperate Dan.

But Duggie James was a thief, and anyway, this money was Mrs Schofield's affair; she could give it to whoever she liked and she'd chosen Henry. If it hadn't been for him that little leather bag might be still in Spring Mill, or at the bottom of the canal.

Two hundred pounds. It wouldn't buy a dream kitchen but it was a start, and at least they could get the Gas Board to come and look at the cooker. It had begun exploding when you lit the back burners, and Mrs Hooper was getting too nervous to touch it. And he could buy a bike too, if he wanted. There was no end to the possibilities represented by that crisp blue cheque.

'Keep it dark,' warned Noreen's Fred, rattling up in his van after breakfast. 'It's fabulous news, mate, but do keep quiet about it. If it gets into the papers people'll be round cadging. That's what always happens when someone gets rich.'

Apart from being pleased, Mrs Hooper hardly said anything about the two hundred pounds, except that it was *his*, to do what he liked with. Henry was hanging on to his mother. She'd never left his side after the canal episode, not for days and days. Now if it had been their Graham's money Mrs Snell would have put it straight in a building society for him, till he got married.

26

It was odd but the money didn't make any difference to Henry. Within twenty-four hours he'd spent that cheque so many times, in his mind, that he was totally confused. He decided to let his mother look after it, till he knew what he wanted. It was too much to take in all at once. Something else happened anyway, something that put the whole thing out of his head.

It was his first day back at school after being ill. 'If you feel up to it, Hen,' Noreen said at breakfast, 'we'll take you down to the Art Centre in the van. The exhibition's being taken down today. You do want to see it, don't you?'

Henry was embarrassed. He'd forgotten all about her 'sculpt'. In the drama of Hunt The Blob, and falling in the canal, the spine-chilling creation being so frantically assembled on the other side of the wall had gone clean out of his mind. He went red when he realized. For all her odd ways he'd become extremely fond of Cousin Noreen. Most people were odd anyway.

'Did you win then?' he said in a tiny voice.

'I – I did quite well,' she said modestly, glancing at Fred, and glowing slightly under the floury make-up. 'You'll see, this afternoon. But we must get there before they touch it.'

Henry agreed to come, but he wasn't going to the Platt Art Centre in his purple horrors. When he got home from school he ran straight upstairs to get his jeans on.

'Hurry *up*,' Noreen shouted, quite bossily for her. She seemed very anxious to be off; she kept peeping through the front curtains and so did his mother, who was off work yet again; and Fred was already revving his rainbow van up, outside the front door.

They bundled Henry into the back while he was still doing up his trousers. 'What's the big hurry?' he grumbled. 'Don't *push*, Noreen, honestly. Anyway, isn't my mum coming?' She'd gone back inside and shut the door.

'No, she's been round the exhibition. Anyway, she's got somebody coming to see her.'

It was Henry's dad. He was walking slowly up the drive of Fir Grove, pushing a bike. Fred nearly knocked him over as they whizzed down towards the gates. Noreen waved madly at him, and Mr Hooper waved back.

'*Hey!*' Henry shouted to Fred. 'Stop, will you, that's my father. I've not seen him for months, I want – STOP!' He'd only caught a brief glimpse of him as they rattled by. He was thinner in the face, and a bit sad-looking.

'You're very like him, Hen,' Noreen observed calmly, turning round in her seat and staring.

'Yes. But I wanted to see him. It's *important*.' Henry tried to keep his voice level but he couldn't. He pressed his nose against the window and tears came into his eyes as his father turned into a little black dot, and disappeared.

'All right, all right, we'll be coming straight back, and when we do he'll still be there. Now just have faith in your Auntie Noreen. OK?'

'OK,' Henry muttered, rubbing at his face and feeling about two and a half. He felt so mixed up at the sight of his father he didn't know what was happening to him any more.

'You see, if we don't go straight down, mate, we'll miss the perishing exhibition, then she'll be *hurt*, you know what she's like,' and Fred grinned, and wagged a thumb at Noreen. She grinned back slyly.

Henry noticed. Noreen wasn't the type to get 'hurt'. It was obviously a plot, and they were all in it together. It was nothing to do with her masterpiece; it was to do with his parents.

'But are you sure he'll *wait*?' he said anxiously, as they slowed down for the traffic lights on Jubilee Road.

'I'm quite sure.'

'Did he have a suitcase?' A tiny seed of hope had put down its roots in Henry's heart, but he still wasn't banking on anything, not yet.

'A *suitcase*? On a *bike*? No, well, I don't think so. Why? Is he a travelling salesman or something?' and she giggled.

'No,' Henry said stonily. She knew perfectly well what he was getting at; she was just in a daft mood. 'No, he works in the Council Offices.' Well, he did do. After all that leave of absence, and going away to 'think things out', and trips to Paris with crazy Uncle Bill, he might well have been given the sack, and that'd be two of them, if Mum didn't stick with the *Examiner*. They were a right pair. If Dad did come back they might need Henry's two hundred pounds.

He didn't ask Noreen anything else but as soon as he'd had a quick, polite look at her sculpt he was going straight home. He'd got to see his father while he had the chance.

There were queues of traffic all the way into the town centre. By the time they arrived the exhibition had been more or less dismantled but Noreen's entry was still intact, all on its own in the middle of the second-floor gallery, a light, high-ceilinged room that smelt of new paint. Down below, through thick double-glazing, red buses lumbered in uncanny silence round Darnley town centre.

'Go and have a look at it, Henry,' Noreen whispered. 'Tell me what you think.' She'd gone all nervous now and she wouldn't come with him; she just sat down with Fred under the 'Exit' sign, on a yellow plastic bench surrounded with rubber plants.

Henry walked across the glossy tiled floor, his rubber soles squeaking. The 'sculpt' was white, all white, because the whole thing had been sprayed with thick glossy paint and it was mounted on a board the size of a double bed.

He stared at it. He could see how she'd used all his junk – all the familiar shapes were there, the rounded bobbles of the egg box cartons, the jagged spikes of nails and screws, and the wire coat-hangers arranged in bunches, like murderous fans. The rubbish had been transformed into a churning white sea and on top of it was a misshapen pyramid, cut, he

could see, from hacked-about polystyrene packing, collected from the Jubilee Road dustbins on Tuesday afternoons.

Sticking out of it all was his leg. It was at an angle, not vertical, but lolling sideways, as if it was forever sinking into the icy sea below. The foot was in place again but put on all lopsided, as if some crazy surgeon had performed a midnight operation on it with needle and thread. And something was running down from the join in thick streaks. Was it glue perhaps? Or paint? Or was it meant to be blood? It was white like everything else, the whole thing was this awful white. It was hurting his eyes.

He stood and looked at it for a very long time. In spite of the leg, sticking up like that, and the coat-hangers, and the egg boxes, nothing about it made him want to laugh, or even smile. It filled him with a strange, inexplicable *empty* feeling, and a coldness. The impact was quite uncanny. Eventually Noreen crept up behind him. 'Well, what do you think of it, Henry?' she said, still very nervous.

Henry didn't know what to say. 'What . . . what does it *mean* exactly?' he said at last. 'Has it got a title?'

She indicated a printed card with her foot, and he bent down and read it. 'Noreen Elizabeth Clegg, 16s to 18s, First Class Commendation.' Then he saw the title. *Afterwards*.

'*Afterwards*?' he repeated, reading it again. 'After *what* though? I don't get it, Noreen. What does it mean?' But he was finding, now, that he couldn't take his eyes off what she had created, out of all his bits of junk.

Fred had strolled across the room and was looking at it with them. 'What does it *mean*?' Noreen repeated slowly, holding his big drummer's hand. 'It depends on the person, Henry. It could mean a lot of things.'

Then he said suddenly, 'Is it after The Bomb?'

He was thinking of that awful 'comic' book Fred had shown him months ago, and about the great winter that might come upon the whole world, if They dropped it, when the sun would no more give its light, and when nothing would grow or flourish ever again. Henry's leg was all that remained of the human race, and that too was sinking, into the terrible sea.

'Well, *is* it?' he repeated. He was glued to Noreen's creation now, and it was doing the strangest, sickliest things to his insides.

Noreen scratched her head and looked at it with him. 'It could be,' she said at last, 'but it didn't *start* like that, Henry; I just wanted to do something with all that rubbish of yours. It inspired me. The leg came into it afterwards. It doesn't have to *mean* anything anyway, does it? It means whatever you think it means. That's what matters.'

27

The Arts Centre people wanted to go home and they were getting awkward about Fred dismantling the 'sculpt'. They were rushing him and they also wanted it to go down the back stairs. Even so, the whole operation was going to take a considerable time, and the roads were choked now, with home-going traffic. Henry said he'd walk back. He didn't want to wait.

He could still see *Afterwards* quite clearly, in his mind's eye, as he pushed his way through the shoppers towards Jubilee Road; in fact, he simply couldn't get that eerie spine-chilling creation out of his head. The leg sticking up out of the top should have been dead funny really, but it had frightened Henry. It looked so helpless.

The 'sculpt' wasn't about The Bomb to him, not really; it was more about how people felt. It was about his memory of Grandma Clegg at Grandad's funeral and about old Nellie Schofield fighting to clear her dead husband's name. It was about himself, the pain in his heart the night of The Row, when Dad had walked out and left Mum weeping at the kitchen table. It was about all the emptiness and need and want inside him now. It was about everything.

It was Tuesday, rubbish night in Jubilee Road, and all the bins were out as usual, lined up outside the shops like rows of elderly Daleks. Alice Modes' windows were plastered with notices: 'Monster Sale' and 'Everything Must Go'. They were obviously closing down. Perhaps the publicity from the Schofield affair hadn't done them any good, or perhaps they'd just given up trying to persuade people to dress in 1950s fashions. Where would Eunice Snell go now?

The new delivery-boy, serving his time till the end of the month, was gloomily sweeping the pavement and kicking boxes together. He'd been at it again, obviously, chopping away at the poor fashion models. One of the big cartons had a single arm sticking out of it now like someone drowning.

Henry saw it but he wasn't even tempted; he just walked on steadily. He wasn't interested at that moment, and he wasn't sure that he ever would be again. He wanted to know what was happening at home, not lumber himself with useless rubbish. He'd leave that arm to Desperate Dan, or perhaps Noreen could do something with it. Somehow, rubbish didn't excite him any more.

When he reached Fir Grove he went up the drive very slowly, with his eyes on his feet, hardly daring to look up in case the bike had gone. In the end he was standing on the front step, so he had to look. There it was, under the bay window, and his father was opening the door and saying hello.

'Do you like Noreen's sculpture?' Mrs Hooper asked him, coming out too. 'She did well, didn't she?'

'Yes,' replied Henry, but his voice was very muffled because his dad was hugging him hard. He really didn't want to think about *Afterwards* any more. It was Now that concerned him.

All that terrible empty whiteness inside him, all that longing, was giving way to a warm comfortable feeling as he walked into the house, guarded on both sides like some Very Important Person. It reminded him of being propped up in the hall by Mum and Noreen, the night Mrs Snell had arrived with the hedgehogs. At least he wouldn't be looking for those any more.

He'd got plenty of money now, he'd got The Reward. The odd thing was, though, that he didn't really want it; all that effort and he couldn't think what to spend it on.

They went into the kitchen and his mother put the kettle on and took three cups and saucers down from the dresser. It looked quite hopeful. She then produced an amazing sunken fruit cake from a tin. Mum's cakes always sank, and Dad liked eating the sticky part in the middle with a spoon. It had always been his 'treat'.

Henry looked at them both, and loved them. If only Dad would stay; that was what he wanted most of all. It was all he'd ever wanted.